Demonic Visions
50 Horror Tales

I0741844

Demonic Visions 50 Horror Tales

© 2015

ISBN-13: 978-0-9861114-0-2

Foreword by the Editor

Welcome to volume one of the Demonic Visions series. You are about to embark upon a literary journey unlike any you have taken before. The horror tales featured in this book were selected from nearly a thousand submissions, by authors located all over the world. Every future volume of the Demonic Visions series will include new writings by each of these authors. Our writers include both the established, and new up and coming talent. These tales have only one thing in common: I found each of them to be wickedly delightful! So enjoy, and I hope that you will join us for the entire Demonic Visions saga which is intended to last many, many years and span many, many volumes…

~Chris Robertson, author of *Death Dreams Deluxe*

Cover art by Steve Wenta, artwork on Facebook: *Visions of Dislocation - the art of Steve Wenta*

Lettering and visual effects by Grant Cross, artwork on Facebook: *Grant Cross Artwork*

Table of Contents

1. ROOM SERVICE
Michael Schomaker

Jonathan felt the dampness and the cold as he lay within a corner of the dark basement. His dark hair dripped sweat as he lay there, shaking. In his right hand he clutched a piece of broken glass, holding it so tightly that blood dripped from his palm. He opens his eyes and reveals the milky white scar upon his right iris, which appeared to tear right through the brownish hue.

Jonathan sits up, breathing heavily and still trembling. He reaches across his body with the piece of glass and begins cutting into his wrist. The blood drips from his wound and pools upon the cement floor. "I can't. I can't do this anymore," he mumbles to himself, and then stops the cutting. He stands upright and drops the glass and watches it shatter onto the basement floor.

In the distance a woman cries out, "Help me. Why are you doing this?" She sits within a cell of steel built into the basement. Her only clothing is a blood covered blue nighty which hardly covers her body, and her hands are handcuffed to her feet. With a voice that displays her distress she cries out, "Just let me go."

Jonathan turns away from her and starts toward the stairs. He is a pale man, well built, wearing nothing but black pants. He steps upon his own blood with bare feet as he walks. The woman watches and cries as he walks up the stairs and opens the door. The bright light from upper floor blinds her momentarily as he leaves the basement. Then as fast as she blinks her eyes he is gone and it is dark again. Jonathan shuts the door behind him with the sickening knowledge that this will not be the last time he visits the basement before morning.

The sun rises the next day and shines its rays upon the windows of a nearby hotel. The drapes of the grand French door blow mightily with a gust of wind. Inside, a heavyset Latina woman grabs the French doors and slams them shut. Her pink and white maid's outfit displays a nametag reading "Rosa" hand written upon a piece of tape. She turns and views the unkempt room, clothes strewn across the floor and a suitcase full of garments on the bed.

"Its past check out time and her shit is still in here," she says to herself in a thick Spanish accent. Rosa leaves the room hastily with her maid cart and slams the door closed. "Management's going to hear about this." She turns and marches down the hallway of an upscale hotel. As she rounds the corner another employee knocks upon a nearby room of the hotel.

"Room service," a pale, well-built man calls out just before he opens the door and enters the room.

As Rosa arrives at the front desk she calls out, "Another guest is staying past check out. Did she pay for another night Danny?" The man behind the desk turns to the computer and starts typing. "Calm down Rosa," he mutters. "Maybe they just forgot." Rosa turns and walks away while Danny continues to type. He just shakes his head.

Rosa returns to her assigned hallway and pushes her cleaning cart onward. The other man now exits the room he had been in. "John, Jonathan did you get that room done?" Rosa sarcastically asks.

As he crosses the threshold the hall lights illuminate his pale face and the scar upon his right eye. "Yes" he answers. "It's done." Jonathan pushes his cart down the hallway and turns around a corner. As he does so, a woman's hand falls from the curtain beneath the cart and drags across the floor. He glances back toward Rosa and sees that she is looking the other way.

Jonathan uses his foot to push the female hand back under the cart, and moves quickly toward the service elevator. As he pushes the cart into the elevator he presses the button marked "B". A blood stained bandage upon his wrist is revealed, and he quickly pulls the cuff of his grey uniform down to conceal it.

Night has fallen when Jonathan returns home. He pulls a large, heavy bag from the trunk of his car, and struggles a bit as he drags it up to the house. Around back he stops near a small round door at the base of the foundation, and drops the bag upon the door. The hinges bend beneath the weight as the small portal consumes the bag, and snaps shut again.

Inside the basement the bag begins to move. Timidly, the shaking finger nail of a woman protrudes from the plastic. She stretches the bag open far enough to see the room through her fuzzy and watering eyes. She sees then a woman laying hands bound to feet upon the floor. She is wearing a bloody blue nighty.

"Hello, hey help me!" she both shouts and whispers at the same time. She gathers up the strength to sit despite her hands being bound with duct tape. She takes a closer look at the woman on the ground and now sees that she lies within a pool of blood. With this sight comes the feeling of absolute terror, which quickly takes over her body. When her vision starts to clear, the full gruesomeness of the scene is revealed. The woman's head is resting on a cement block with a large blood covered rock beside it. Her head has been cracked open as if it were a soft melon, and the contents of her skull are simply gone.

As she starts to scream in terror, a hand reaches from out of the darkness and covers her mouth. She fights against his grasp but Jonathan holds her too tightly. He whispers into her ear and her eyes flex wide with horror.

"I don't like to do this," he says and pauses to look down. "I don't like it. I don't like anything about it… but I have to eat. I have been cursed to live undead for hundreds of years… perhaps infinity. We go by many names: walking dead, the undead, zombies… We walk among you and none of you realize it. Eating human brain tissue reverses the rot of my own flesh."

She realizes with even greater horror that he has told this to many people before her.

"They have no idea," he continues. "The living that is, until the uncontrollable hunger takes us over. Then we must feed. And I'm hungry." The woman closes her eyes as tears well up and then pour down her cheeks. Jonathan reaches back and takes a large rock in hand, and then hurls it downward upon her head.

2. A TASTE FOR LIFE
Patrick Freivald

"And how old were you when you died, Mister Beauchamp?" Joan Rothman asked, leaning back in her chair. The scientists watched her behind the one-way mirror, hands clasped behind their backs.

"Twenty-seven," the corpse replied, more gurgle than speech, as it gazed idly around the interview room. Joan jotted down the response, then chewed pensively on the tip of her red pen. The lights flickered as the air circulators shuddered to life in the depths of the bunker, filling the observation room with a faint scent of bleach and formaldehyde.

She crossed her legs and rested the clipboard between her knee and the folding table, unknowingly flashing her slip to the men behind the mirror. Bhim Raychaudhuri smiled appreciatively at the view and spoke into the microphone wired to her ear bead. "Math, Miss Rothman."

"Thank you," she said to the creature, making no sign that she'd heard the command. "And how old are you now?" She poised the pen above the clipboard.

The corpse scowled, the pallid flesh of its forehead wrinkling in concentration under the single naked bulb. "What year is it?"

"It's twenty sixty-seven, Mister Beauchamp."

"What month?" it asked.

"April, Mr. Beauchamp. On the surface it's springtime."

"And I died in two thousand twelve?" it asked, wheezing.

"As near as we can tell, Mister Beauchamp."

It grunted, a flatulent gasp of rotten breath, and scowled down at its manacled hands. It shifted its weight in the folding chair, and its good eye lolled up to look at her face. "I'm hungry."

She nodded. "Food is coming. Please be patient, Mr. Beauchamp."

"Real food?" the corpse asked, leaning forward in anticipation. Joan didn't answer. Her eyes flicked toward the mirror.

Behind the glass, Bhim took off his spectacles and polished them as he turned to his partner. "Well, it looks like the memory recovery works."

Mike Reed nodded reluctantly. "Yeah, I suppose, if you remind it who it is all the time.

But they still can't do simple arithmetic." He stretched one crooked finger towards the mirror. "Look at it, our most promising subject, fidgeting and hiding behind the hunger to avoid answering the question. That's pretty disappointing."

"Baby steps, Mike. Last time he couldn't even remember his name."

Mike shoved his finger under Bhim's nose. "Don't you 'baby step' me, Bhim. The time before it remembered its name and calculated its age! Is two-digit subtraction too much to ask?"

Bhim chuckled. "No, but that time he also tried to feed on Joan after three minutes of questioning. Look!" He pointed at the analog clock hanging on the wall. "It's been nearly twenty minutes, and he's only now beginning to show the signs. The serum works."

They turned their attention back to the room, where Joan kept nervously glancing in their direction. The men sighed in unison.

"Okay," Mike said. "Feed it and get it back to its cage. We'll try Mister Lamandola."

Four months later, Mister Beauchamp sat at the same table, staring uninterestedly at the voluptuous form of Joan Rothman. Bhim's grin was infectious, but Mike possessed strong antibodies to good humor.

Mike grabbed the microphone and barked, "Tell it to stop stalling and tell us!"

Joan cringed at the volume, then composed herself. She reached across the table and supportively squeezed the dead thing's hand. "Please, Mister Beauchamp. It's been nine weeks since you've fed. How often do you think about it?"

It lifted its dead eye and regarded her flatly. It licked its lips, an all too human gesture with no biological purpose. "All the time, Miss Rothman. All the time. It's hard to think about anything else."

Behind the mirror, Mike grunted. "You see? It's like a child molester. All we've done is suppress it."

"Hush," Bhim said.

"Really?" Joan asked. "Even now, when I was reading to you? After all this time we've spent together?"

Beauchamp's lips peeled back, revealing black, rotten teeth; a smile. "It consumes me."

"But you control it," she said, slowly retracting her hand. "Why?"

"It makes me human," he replied. "Your serum. It makes the urge... Not less, but somehow controllable. I don't need it anymore. I just want it."

Bhim didn't need to look at Mike to feel the 'I told you so' eyes boring into his skull.

"What about the food we give you, Mister Beauchamp? Meat? Bread? Water?" Joan asked.

"Call me Jason." It wasn't a request.

"Ok, Jason, what about the food we give you? Doesn't it satisfy you?"

Jason shook his head. A clump of hair tumbled to the floor.

"Increased physical degeneration," Mike said.

"Shut up!" Bhim replied. "I'm trying to listen."

"...like it. Do you like steak?" it asked.

Joan nodded.

The zombie gurgled. "I used to love steak. All food, really. I was a chef..." It stared at her longingly.

Joan tapped the intercom twice. She was getting nervous.

"But now?" she asked. Outwardly, she was cool as ice.

"Now it all tastes like nothing." It continued to leer at her with its good eye, its bad eye drifting lazily around the room. "I move, but I don't live. I don't taste anything. I can't feel anything. But that's not the worst of it..."

She tapped the intercom again. "What's the worst of it, Jason?"

"Shouldn't we--" Mike started.

"Shush!" Bhim's eyes didn't twitch from the scene in front of him.

It hesitated. "The worst of it..." It froze. Joan waited. "The worst is that I don't want anything. Anything at all."

The intercom clicked again, twice. "So the serum works, Jason?" she asked. "You said you don't need to feed now."

"I don't need to. Haven't for weeks. I'm not mindless, you know."

She smiled at him.

Here it is, Bhim thought.

"What would you do if we set you free, Jason?"

"That's simple," it said. "I'd kill you all. And then I'd eat your brains."

Mike screamed in frustration.

Bhim chuckled despondently. "We're never getting out of this bunker, are we?"

3. THE G.A.T.E.
James Pratt

"Get that generator going!" Crichton, the chief physicist, demanded. His shock of white hair in disarray, he looked more like a mad scientist than ever.

Sweat gleaming on his bare scalp, Pyle, Crichton's team lead, shot him a dirty look. "I'm trying! Maintenance should be doing this!"

"A doctorate in theoretical physics and you can't get a generator working…" Crichton paused and took a deep breath. "They locked themselves in the bomb shelter after the alarms went off. Besides, they're not even allowed in the lab. We have to take care of this ourselves."

"No shit," Pyle said as he screwed the enormous generator's gas cap back on. "And hold that flashlight steady."

"Why do you think the maintenance crew did that?" Kessler, the pudgy lead programmer, asked, never taking his eyes off the G.A.T.E. Other than the flashlight, the artifact was the only source of illumination in the converted airplane hangar that served as their laboratory. "Hole themselves up, I mean."

The right corner of Crichton's mouth curled slightly upward, the closest he ever came to a smile. "I'm sure they've spent a fair amount of time speculating about what we're trying to do in here. Who knows what they came up with?"

"What are we trying to do?" Kessler asked. "I mean besides the obvious."

"We'll know when we know," Crichton replied. "Frankly, I didn't think we'd get this far."

"Let's see now," Pyle murmured, studying the nobs and switches that covered the generator's control panel. "I think it needs to be primed somehow."

Kessler glanced at the rack of blank monitor screens. "Kind of weird that the power would go out and the UPS would fail exactly twenty four hours practically to the second after the G.A.T.E. opened."

"Weird," Crichton conceded, "but not beyond the realm of possibility."

Pyle grunted. "I guess the backup generator wasn't such a bad idea after all."

Crichton handed him the instruction manual. "It would've been even better idea if you'd read this first."

"I figured the maintenance crew would handle it," Pyle muttered as he flipped through the manual.

While the other two argued, Kessler's gaze drifted back to the G.A.T.E. Ten feet high at its apex, the strange characters etched into the archway's smooth, ceramic-like surface emitted a pale, eerie glow. After reading the reports of its discovery in the shadow of the Phobos Monolith where it had sat orbiting the planet Mars for thousands, possibly millions of years, he'd called in every favor he was owed to secure a spot on the research team. Overseeing the group of programmers who had coded E.V.E., the revolutionary AI which allowed their computers to communicate with the G.A.T.E. and bring it back to life, Kessler had proven his worth.

Kessler wanted to approach the G.A.T.E. but hesitated. As a dormant relic, it had been a fascinating specimen. Awake was another matter.

"Now that it's open, should we be wearing radiation suits?" Kessler asked.

Crichton shook his head. "We already checked it with a Geiger counter, remember? Nothing's coming out of it, radiation or otherwise. Not even a single graviton to imply the presence of matter. It's a void, just like I expected."

"I still think a kill switch would have been a good idea," Pyle said. "We can't shut the thing down till E.V.E.'s back online."

"We couldn't take the chance of an uncontrolled shutdown," Crichton replied. "You know that."

"If there's no danger, then what's the hurry of getting E.V.E. back online?" Pyle asked.

"This lab's airtight," Crichton reminded him. "When the power went out, the ventilation system shut off. There's a…slight chance our remaining oxygen is being sucked through the G.A.T.E."

Pyle started to say something when he noticed Kessler standing before the G.A.T.E. "Kessler, what are you doing?"

"What do you think is in there?" Kessler asked as he gazed into the fathomless black framed within the archway.

"Nothing," Crichton said. "It's hyperspace, or the void between universes or whatever you want to call it. It's literally nothing."

"That's just your theory," Kessler replied.

"Don't get too close," Pyle cautioned. "The magnetic shield's down, remember?"

"It could be anything," Kessler said, a hint of awe in his voice. "Anything at all."

"Kessler, get away from there," Crichton said.

"Why?" Kessler asked. "You said there wasn't any danger."

"Theoretically yes but there's no way of-"

Kessler froze. "Something's in there."

"What?"

"There's something in there, moving in the darkness."

"Impossible," Crichton huffed. "It's debatable there's even a 'there' in there."

Kessler leaned closer. "I...I can see..."

"What?" Crichton demanded. "What can you see?"

"Hold the flashlight steady!" Pyle growled.

"Explosions of color," Kessler said. "And shapes-"

A sudden burst of light erupted from the G.A.T.E., momentarily illuminating the room.

"Christ!" Pyle cried, rubbing his eyes.

"Christ," Crichton said as another burst of light lingered just long enough to reveal a second Kessler standing beside a horrified first.

But it wasn't Kessler. It was an alternate Kessler; slack-jawed, tumorous, and with pale, milky eyes, it was the Kessler of an anti-universe where life was death and death was life.

Crichton struck Pyle with the flashlight. "Get the generator on!"

"Jesus!" Pyle protested.

Crichton was squinting at the G.A.T.E. when a third burst of light revealed that Kessler, their Kessler, was gone but the other one remained. It turned its awful gaze toward them, revealing a fist-sized polyp on its left cheek.

"Pyle," whispered as the anti-Kessler took a shuffling step.

"Got it!" Pyle cried as the generator kicked on, immediately followed by the lights and the comforting hum of the ventilation system. "What do you-?" Pyle gasped at the sight of the anti-Kessler.

A three-second buzz heralded the magnetic shields coming online, surrounding the G.A.T.E. in an invisible, impenetrable field, and the anti-Kessler vanished.

"Did you...see that?" Pyle asked after a moment.

"Yes."

"Kessler's gone," Pyle observed.

"I know."

"What do we do?" Pyle asked.

"Contact HR and tell them we need a new programmer."
"You're an asshole, Crichton."
"I know."

4. LOST ALLEYS
Jeffrey Thomas

There are places within cities that only the drunk, drugged or insane can find. Even if you have been there before you will not find them again if sober – assuming that you are one of those who occasionally regains sobriety. The angles and geometry, the very lay-out of the buildings and the infrastructure, conspire to direct you elsewhere to more prosaic destinations. It may be that this design is intentional. Streets point you past these alleys, and more conventional passageways bend eye and foot beyond these narrow sub-alleys. Magician's misdirection and the psychology of art — but also our fear and inhibition of straying from the path – keep these places hidden.

I have found such secret or forgotten corners within several cities; I am usually able to remember what I saw at these places, but not always the name of the city in which I saw them. Often in the morning, I cannot remember immediately the city in which I've awoken.

I suppose my proclivity for finding these shadowy caverns within the mountain ranges of each metropolis I visit has to do with the fact that I am usually either drunk or drugged, and perhaps perpetually insane.

Somehow this night I had found my way back to a courtyard I had visited before in my somnambulistic wanderings. You never actually forget anything; your mind simply blots out what is unnecessary, or unwanted. But part of me must have wanted to return to see another of the battles in this tiny arena.

The walls were of brick, and stretched high, windowless. Perhaps it had been a great chimney; there was a black iron door, low to the ground. They kept some of the contestants in there. That other night, I had watched an Asian dwarf battle a thylacine, one of those supposedly extinct Tasmanian tiger-wolves. Crates and cinder-blocks piled shoulder-high enclosed the ring of fighting. When I arrived that night, several dozen dark forms encircled the ring.

I can't stand cruelty to animals; I had been glad when the thylacine won. I stood back smoking a cigarette until more of the willing opponents were brought out. These two had made a decision to enter voluntarily into the ring. Not necessarily a rational decision, but they were not unwilling victims. Well, victims yes, of many unknown tortures from without and within, but they were not on this night deprived of their free will.

They were two naked men. One was tall and skeletal, the other short and thin also. The tall one wore brass knuckles with spikes on one hand, and in the other gripped a baling hook. His opponent held a railroad spike and a broken bottle with the neck taped up, so as to function as a handle. The short one was a black man, and had blacker keloids of scar tissue, mostly upon his face, but I was uncertain if they were decorative or the healed wounds of exhibitions past.

I infiltrated the crowd and insinuated myself close to the ring's barrier. Someone squeezed my ass but when I punched his bloated face, the act was not repeated. By this time the battle had begun.

The gladiators sprang away from one another, the tall one swinging his brass-knuckled fist up into his own face, the short warrior gouging his bottle into his own inner thigh while pounding the dull chisel-point of the spike into his sternum. I leaned onto the wall; I'd never seen a sight such as this before.

No one cheered them on. The spectators stood in their drug-like states, silently beholding the spectacle. Even the dying did not scream. A man in a three-piece suit on my right clutched foreign-looking money within his fist, whispering encouragement to one of fighters in a language I found unrecognizable.

The tall one had hooked himself in the leg and tore upward with horrendous jerks. His blood appeared blackened as it sprayed upon his cadaverous skin. But now the black man charged him, linked arms with the man and wrestled him to the ground. The tall man's ripped leg appeared to be too damaged to resist the force. The black man got his arms around both of the other's and forced his face into the ground. Holding the tall man's arms inside his elbows left the black man's hands free to jab his bottle under his own jaw. The apparent victor then halted the assault upon his foe, and inexplicably began hammering deep gashes into his own dark skin.

I understood the game then, as the revelation came upon me. The combatants were to combat themselves; one had to inflict more damage upon himself than the other could likewise do to his body, while preventing the other – without harming him – from mutilating himself.

The black man had taken charge quickly, perhaps a running champion. But now the tall one twisted halfway free, and had extricated the baling hook from his leg. The emaciated creature swung it up into his throat, and then tore it free with indifference. I heard a hiss of approval from the spectators, and the hiss of spraying blood.

The black man bore all his mass down upon the other's arm (he apparently wasn't allowed to let go of either weapon to use his hands) but the wound was already too wide. The tall man quickly became as dark as the black man, as best as I could tell in the dim light. I felt a damp mist on my hand. The tall man convulsed under the smaller. Ah, now I knew. The black man wasn't the running champion, but the running loser, and the fight with one's self had been to the death.

There were more contests. Two spirited adolescents, that I could have more easily imagined playing a video game, were next. Then two men wrestling to rape each other. A man in a wheelchair with a spear versus two pit bulls that had been firmly lashed together in opposite directions. All three lost, I understand, but I had then turned away to do the drugs I had brought with me.

I awoke inside a dark place. I realized it was the place behind that black iron door. Panic came over me. Surely they were going to use me in an upcoming match! But then I could vaguely recall crawling into that space, and falling asleep there. When I pushed at the door it opened on creaking rusty hinges.

There was a square of light at the top of the chimney, and though the shaft was blue with shadowed gloom, I was startled at the relative brightness of day. I was afraid to emerge from my safe tomb, but did so anyway. The arena was empty except for an obese man with a shaven head inside the ring, spray-painting over the dried blood. He just glanced at me. I wandered around the outside of the ring, between it and the walls of the chimney. I circled as though lost in a spiral maze, smoking a broken cigarette I had found.

I sat against the brick wall, pulled my knees up close, waiting for night to come. I couldn't leave, you understand, until darkness fell. It was daylight. I was sober. I didn't know the way.

5. CIGARETTES AND MURDER
Kerry G.S. Lipp

"No thanks, I don't smoke," Clayton said waving the offered pack away with his hand.

"If you can't smoke a cigarette you can't kill a person. It's really that simple," I said.

I didn't move my hand away. Instead, pack still in hand, I punched him as hard as I could in the middle of his chest. Ever taken a bone on bone shot to the sternum? It hurts. He gaped at me. Pain in his eyes, but to his credit, he caught himself quick and got an inch from my face. He wasn't going to hit me, but he wasn't backing down either. Maybe there was hope for Clay after all.

"Take one rookie," I said and after he looked me hard in the eye for a full few seconds, he relented.

The sigh of disappointment from the guy taped to the chair was like a sonic boom. Like the poor bastard thought we were going to forget all about him and kill each other. Like he'd be able to get free.

I gave our prisoner a look and he squirmed and shook his head, the duct tape over his mouth drowning out his words.

"I promise it's for a purpose Clayton," I said and fished my lighter out of my pocket. I lit mine first and then, even though he flinched, Clayton let me light his.

I stared at Clay, eyes cutting through him like a medieval sword, and making sure he was taking the smoke into his lungs and not just into his mouth. His eyes widened and poked out a bit and then he went into a short fit of coughing. He looked half sick, half ready to throw a punch. I grabbed the wrist holding the cig and raised it back to his lips.

"Again," I said.

He looked at me, face contorted, still trying to handle the coughing fit. With icy eyes flaming into my guts he took another drag.

"Keep smoking that cigarette, don't you dare stop. And keep watching me, don't you dare look away," I said.

He kept smoking and he kept watching as I pulled out my gun and placed it to the center of our captive's forehead. I looked back at Clay and liked what I saw, but the test wasn't over yet.

"Clay." He just stared back at me, intense, eyes staring not through me, but into me. He hit the smoke and tried to smile through a gag. "Don't you fucking dare look away."

I removed the duct tape from the captive's mouth and he started whining about how he had a family and how he was sorry and all the same old bullshit. It was disgusting. I looked at Clay while the man blabbered. The man continued to beg. Please I'm sorry I didn't mean to blah blah blah. I've heard it all a million times.

Still holding the gun to the prisoner's forehead, I looked at Clay, I had to keep looking, had to make sure he was still smoking that cigarette.

"You alright Clay?" I asked.

"Never better," he coughed out.

"Good," I said and pulled the trigger and blew the guy's brains all over the floor. There wasn't a wall behind him.

Clay flinched a little, but that was forgivable. The shot was loud and the sight was gruesome. Most people, even people looking to get into this business, have never seen anything remotely close to this before. Between the flying brains and the cigarette smoke, I was just happy Clay didn't blow his groceries.

I lowered the pistol, never breaking eyes with Clay, and made a show of inhaling the pistol smoke and the brain smell.

Clay looked at me with several questions in his eyes.

I looked at his smoke, it was down to the filter. I nodded, and he tossed it to the floor and stomped it with the heel of his boot.

I walked out to the truck and brought him a broom and dustpan and a mop and bucket and some cleaning chemicals.

"Clean it up," I said to his green face. "I'll go over it all when you're done, so don't and I mean FUCKING DON'T miss anything," I said grabbing his collar, making sure I touched him where I'm sure the bruise from earlier was. I didn't hate him and I wasn't mad at him, but acting like this was important. I had to establish authority and make sure he understood how crucial this job really was.

"Got it," he said.

"Good. I'll be out in the truck lining up the next job. I like you Clay. A lot. You don't fuck this up, I think this is going to work."

He nodded and started cleaning.

***

After he finished, I inspected his work and found nothing too questionable. The splinters of bone and the chunks of brain were swept and the blood had been mopped. He'd sawn the body and the chair into pieces and torched them. I watched him the whole time. He acted like a

19

professional, but as I watched him I saw him fight down the urge to vomit several times.

Maybe it was just the cigarette I thought and chuckled to myself.

Finally the body and the chair were nothing but ash on that oil-stained concrete floor.

Other than a single piece of bone the size of my pinky nail, I found nothing wrong with his work. Clay was leagues more thorough than most. A keeper. I nodded to him and we left the building and got into the truck.

"You did good," I said and held out my pack of smokes. He nodded and then eyed me up and down before he finally took one and placed it between his lips.

We were already driving back down the road when I took one for myself, lit it, and offered him the lighter. He didn't take it.

"So what's up with the cigarettes?" he asked. "That's bullshit."

"So you watch me blow a dude's brains out without blinking and you've got a problem with smoking?"

"You know what I mean man. Why'd you force me to do that?" he asked.

"I'll tell you why," I said. "Cigarettes and murder are the exact same thing."

He looked at me not comprehending, and I remembered when my mentor, Big G, had taught me the same lesson I now taught Clay. Methods and habits for life really do boil down to how you've been trained.

"It's like this Clay," I said.

I'd been giving this speech for a long time.

"Cigarettes and murder are both bad habits. They are both disgusting. They are both gross. Especially the first time. You might even puke. It's actually amazing to me that you didn't. But once you get that taste and feel that urge, you want to try it again. And the second time you try it, it feels a little better, and the third time, even better. Next thing you know, you're hooked on it, and you want to do it more and more, even when you don't really need to. You know you should quit and you don't, it becomes a part of life. And the worst part is, Clay, that one or the other will probably end in your own death," I said.

"Exactly," Clay said and he pulled out his pistol and smiled with the unlit cig dangling from his lips. Then he shot me in the neck. In a race, the bullet beat the spray of my blood through the window, but it didn't really matter. My own cigarette went flying. I ran the truck off the road

20

and tried to flip it, maybe kill us both, but I couldn't and we just sort of puttered out as my blood ran thick and my breath ran thin.

Undamaged, Clay cocked his head at me and took the cigarette from his lips and put it to mine and lit it, giving me one final smoke as I bled out. I was grateful for that. And then he did something that surprised me.

"Your menthols make me sick," he said as he pulled out his own box of lights.

"You're right," he said, taking a deep drag. "It's pretty disgusting the first time," he said, blowing smoke out both nostrils like a dragon.

"Oh and you're right about both getting you killed too," he smirked.

Just another ambitious young fuck thinking he'll live forever I thought before I gurgled for the last time.

And that chipper young fuck smoked a cigarette while he watched me die. Final breath forgotten as it billowed out my open throat, the last thought in my heart was that if he cleaned this scene up as well as the one earlier he'd end up doing alright. But if not, he'd find himself tied to a chair real soon.

6. THE TANK
Rob Smales

Hard.

Cold.

Two things Derek had never associated with his bed before. For just a moment he wondered what had happened to his down comforter and memory foam mattress topper. And his pillow. Where the hell was his pillow?

"I think this one's coming around."

That snapped Derek awake. His eyes popped open and he sat bolt upright.

"Who are you and what are you..." he began, fully intending to finish the question with a shouted 'doing in my room?', but the words died on his lips as he took in his surroundings.

Huge. Circular. Empty, but for the crowd of naked people standing around on the gray, almost shiny floor upon which he lay. It looked to be of the same material that made up the walls of their enclosure; smooth, gray and slightly reflective — more like smoked glass than a mirror.

Hey, he thought, admittedly not wide awake yet. *Why is everybody naked?*

He felt a draft, felt it in places he usually couldn't. He looked down at himself.

"Oh my God!"

His hands flew to cover, cup and protect himself as he scrambled to his feet.

"Why am I naked? Why are *you* naked? Where are —"

Memory hit him right between the eyes and caused a chill to settle into the more dangly bits of him currently nestled in his own palms. Lights. Huge lights in the sky, coming right at him. The engine sputtering, then dying. Screaming in fear as he abandoned the stalled truck in the road and running, running but the lights were so fast... and then it was all blackness.

"Aliens," he whispered, feeling the fear again.

"Okay," said the loud voice that had wakened him in the first place. "Looks like this genius is all caught up. Now, *you* are going to explain to the rest of us just what the hell is going on here."

Derek tracked the voice to its source: a large, thick-waisted man with the look of a college football player maybe a decade past his sell-by date. He was marching through the crowd of eighteen or twenty naked people, gesturing with both hands for them to clear the way. He was either comfortable with his nakedness or was too freaked out by what was going on to care, but he was making no effort to cover himself up; his angry, foot-stomping stride made Derek glad to be stepping out of the way, and all there were to see were his jiggling buttocks.

Beyond him, beyond this crowd of nudists that Derek was suddenly part of, was a lone man, also naked, sitting on the floor. While everyone gathered by one wall of this strange enclosure, he was out toward the middle of the thirty yard circle circumscribed by the smoky, glass-like walls. He sat alone, and next to... was that a pile of dog shit?

"When I woke up, this guy was the only one already awake," the big man said to the crowd, pointing to the seated man. "I asked him about the lights. We *all* saw the lights, right? I asked around, when some of you woke up... anyone *not* see the lights?"

He waited, but no one raised either hand or voice, so he continued. His voice, though loud, shook, and even without knowing the man Derek could tell he was on the very edge of control.

"So we've all been... you know, abducted. By aliens. Right? I mean, it's *gotta* be aliens, right? What else could it be? Well this guy was here before me, was here before all of us. Long enough to have to make *that* — "

The big man pointed at the small, stinking pile the man sat next to, and Derek realized with a shock that his assumption had been incorrect: there were no dogs here.

" — and I think he's been here long enough to know what they want with us. What they're gonna *do* to us. And I think we need to know. Now."

The smaller man stood, also unashamed of his nudity.

"You'll find out. Trust me."

Then he actually smirked. The big man put a hand on his shoulder, almost gently, though Derek could see his knuckles whiten as the grip tightened.

"They gonna probe us?" he said, shaking the shoulder. "Test us? *Breed* with us? What?"

"You'll see," said the smaller man. "You're just too *stupid* not to."

The first punch split his lip, the second knocked him down. The naked crowd, as crowds have always done, gathered around the fight. Derek, at the back of the group, saw one of the smoky walls ripple up near the ceiling, and there was a great booming *thud*.

"Stop!" Derek said, forcing his way through the tightening crowd. "Stop it! Something's happening!"

Another huge *thud* rocked the room just as Derek reached the fight, but it was over. Broken and bloody, the small man crawled across the floor, the big man's attention stolen by the sounds breaking the air. Derek crouched by the crawling man.

"Why did you do that? Provoke him like that?"

"Because I'm smart. I'm a survivor."

The broken man stopped crawling and, to Derek's disgust, scooped up the pile of filth from the floor and began smearing it on his naked skin.

"What the hell are you *doing*?"

"Becoming unappealing," said the man. A huge *crack* rent the air, and he stared at Derek.

"Do you know the story of the one-clawed lobster?"

"What?"

"This guy in a restaurant gets a lobster, but it's only got one claw. 'Where's the other claw?' he says. Waiter says 'He got in a fight in the lobster tank, and lost it.' The guy says 'Well bring me the winner!'"

The roof of the room suddenly lifted away as a taloned arm the size of a telephone pole reached in, plucking the big man from his feet as he screamed.

"We have a winner!" the small man screamed.

Derek began smearing shit on his skin.

7. WHEN THEY TURN ON YOU
Maggie Carroll

The exhibit is not going well. Not even three glasses of Madeira fixes that.

The crowd has thinned to a handful of the ignorant *nouveau riche*, milling like sheep, sipping their wine and talking about light and shadow and color schemes. They know absolutely nothing, but they like to sound informed. It's mindless chatter. The true aficionados have long since departed, disgusted with my meager offerings. I can't blame them. If I wasn't required by the gallery to be here, I'd leave too.

Robert Jansen of the *Sentinel* circles the diminished crowd like a hungry shark, wineglass in hand. I grind my back teeth. Once upon a time when I was nobody, Robert had written rave reviews. Once upon a time, I was "innovative" and "mind-blowing" and "edgy". I made a name for myself, peaked, and have since been on a downward trajectory. Now he's an asshole with a grudge, reviewing my latest work as though I have somehow wronged him personally. He thrives on my misery. Surely he is loving every minute of this disaster.

He finally approaches me, a smarmy grin plastered upon his face. "Leslie!" he cries, like he's not planning my editorial evisceration. He takes my hand, pretending to be a gentleman when he kisses it. "Wonderful display, darling, as usual. It's a pity so many of your patrons seem to have called it an early night."

I force a smile so brightly that my cheeks hurt. "Hello Robert. The crowd does seem a bit thin tonight, doesn't it?" I laugh, a high tinkling giggle fuelled by the wine sloshing in my stomach. "It's a collection of experimental techniques. I suppose not everyone appreciates them."

His grin widens, canines winking at me under the fluorescents. I want to snatch a heavy sculpture from the nearby table and beat him until his head is a toothless ruin. "What's not to like?"

When I pick up the paper the next morning, I know exactly what he thinks is not to like: everything.

***

I slap colors on the canvas and smear them into mud. I need to paint something, but I know it's a lackluster attempt at best. I'm not close to destitute, won't need to resort to peanut butter and carrot sticks anytime soon. But the blank canvases are mocking me. I need to create.

When I'm finished, I hate it. I loathe it with every fiber of my being. It looks like a kindergarten art project. If only I had some macramé and glitter. *Fuck it*, I think. There's a market for everything. Experienced patrons won't look twice at the canvas, but they're not my only customers these days.

Some ignorant sheep will pay to hang it on their wall.

***

The show is another disaster. The gallery's advertising was misprinted. The flyers in town got the date wrong. The newspaper ad had the time wrong. It's not even in the event listing on the gallery's website. The radio gets it right, but no one listens to the radio anymore.

The paintings are awful, and I cringe into my wine every time someone stops to look at them. Of course, Robert is here, my own personal demon refreshed and ready for more torment. There'll be another review tomorrow, lamenting how I've lost my edge, my spark, my innovation. A peddler of tripe and trash. Mainstream and mundane.

I toss back a fresh glass of wine in one swallow and grimace. It wouldn't hurt half as much if it wasn't true.

***

The kindergarten art project leans against a wall in my studio. I should have glued on macaroni. Maybe a pasta happy face would have made it sell. I drink a bottle of Chablis and stare at it. I hate it, I hate it, I hate it…

Rage and wine burn behind my eyes, and boil over. I grab for the box cutter on my table and, screaming epithets, slash the canvas apart. One canvas isn't enough, but there are plenty of other failures mocking me.

I attack everything in sight.

***

As tantrums go, it could have been worse. There are pieces of canvas everywhere, streamers of color that no longer have meaning. I've broken two easels, and paint jars roll everywhere. Somewhere along the way, I laid into my stack of *Sentinel* review clippings, and shreds of newspaper dot the floor.

I push aside shreds of what might have once been a print of my first sale, and scoop a handful of newspaper towards me. Resting atop the pile is Robert's byline. A wide slash neatly bisects his head, leaving only that smarmy smile to mock me.

Stop. Stare. Nervous flutter in my chest. It's coming.

My breath catches.

Inspiration strikes hard and fast.

***

The scariest sound in the world is a shotgun ratcheting shells. Robert's eyes are wide and wild, and he struggles against the knots. It won't do him any good. I still have my Girl Scout merit badge upstairs.

"You shouldn't have turned on me, Robert. Do you remember when you called my work mind-blowing?" I tap his forehead. He flinches back. "No? That's alright, darling. My next piece will refresh your memory."

Robert screams as I set the shotgun against my shoulder, one long continuous "NNNGH!" under the gag. The most inspiring thing he's ever said. I check the canvas behind him one more time; the angle looks good.

I blow his mind right through the back of his fucking skull.

I blow a hole through the canvas too, but repair putty and a new liner will patch that. A few careful touchups, and no one will ever know the difference.

***

I spend a week going over the canvas with a pair of tweezers and a magnifying glass, removing bits of bone and strands of hair. It streaks the design, leaves tiny smears of white in the rust-red. I'm not sure I like the effect, but decide to leave it alone.

It looks much better when I coat it with Shellac and frame it in poplar.

***

The show is a blinding success. The paintings fly off the walls: an hour left and twelve of the fifteen have sold. I watch as a hostess walks to one of the three open paintings and sets a SOLD placard beneath it. Thirteen now.

A bidding war has erupted over "Painting With Shotguns", the *pièce de résistance*. They're babbling about the colors and texture and boldness, nearly falling over themselves to win it. Even the aficionados are frothing like rabid dogs. I pause long enough to hear the next offer. It's a five-digit figure, not a small one. I smile and move away.

Julie Ryder of *The Herald* circles the burgeoning crowd at a sedate pace, wineglass in hand. I keep an eye on her, rehearse what I'm going to say, and make a note to watch the papers in the morning. You never know when they'll turn on you.

8. THAT THING SHE USED TO CALL RING
Johannes Pinter

So hungry! So furiously hungry!

That is all that runs through the remains of her brain, as she limps along the deserted alleyway. *So furiously, furiously hungry! Must eat something now!*

A low moaning catches her attention, and she sees a dog hidden behind a dumpster. A small one. Breed doesn't matter: it's a piece of meat on four legs. Instead of trying to escape it hides, trembling with fear - *an injured leg!*

With all of her speed she rounds the container, grabs the dog's light brown coat with her dirty hands. A second later, she has torn a large piece of meat from its side as it tries to bite her in defense. The animal howls, screams in pain, but it doesn't matter. She buries her face into the wound, takes another bite. And another. *So hungry!*

Then she sees something on her left hand which holds the dog. Something that glitters. She no longer knows that the thing is called Ring. Or that the Ring sits upon a Finger. Or that the Finger sits on a Hand. But she does know that what used to be called Ring glimmers of gold in the early evening sun, with a thin golden line along the center of a whiter material. The light reflected from the ring hits her eye, and does something with her. It makes her suddenly remember a gleam of memory. The light finds its way into her soul for a fleeting moment, bringing out fragments of her past life. A life before she was bitten. A life that was more than only furious hunger.

The blood on her hands draws her back to the new reality. She forgets the ring. She resumes eating the dog which continues to howl and snap at her until it is dead. She throws away the remains and feels the hunger again. The dog was insufficient. It did not extinguish the craving.

She peeks from the alley and sees others running out of a house down the street. They don't see her as she stands within the distant shadows. They reach a car. But the man who tries to unlock it carries bags and a case and cannot find the key. She watches as he sets them down and rummages in his pockets while the boy stands on guard nearby pleading with the man to hurry.

She doesn't hesitate. Starts running as fast as her broken angle will allow. The man doesn't see her and continues digging into his pockets.

But the boy sees the threat approaching and screams. He points, and the man looks up and stiffens with panic. Instead of running he digs more desperately for the key. He finds it and tries to push the button, fingers trembling frantically. The door clicks but it is too late, she is upon them. She pulls the boy close, biting him upon the neck, blood gushing over his Adidas jacket. The man yells, and tries to push her off of him. When succeeding, she takes hold of the father's arm instead. She buries her teeth into it, and tears out muscle and skin. Blood pours onto the asphalt, and the man pushes upon her head, yelling something she does not understand. The same sound over and over again. But she doesn't care, she wants only to eat.

Then she sees something upon the man's hand. Something that glitters. She no longer knows that the thing is called Ring. Or that the Ring sits on a Finger. But she does know that what used to be called Ring glimmers of gold in the final rays of the daylight. It appears identical to her own, has the same thin golden line along the center. The reflecting light finds its way into her soul for another brief moment, drawing out fragments of a past life. She shifts her gaze and looks at the man who peers at her with red-rimmed, terror filled eyes. Somewhere she understands that his tears are not only from the pain of her bite.

She no longer knows what a soul is, or tears, or how it feels to be eaten by your own wife who was bitten by the infected one day prior, so she takes another bite.

She eats all night, there in the street. Doing her best to sooth the fierce craving. But when she leaves the remains of the man and the boy near the car, it doesn't take long before she is hungry again.

Furiously hungry...

9. WATER
Jeani Rector, Editor
The Horror Zine

She felt the dampness in her armpits and thought, *I mustn't sweat.*

How long had it been since her last drink of water? Ashley compulsively checked the cabinet that held small plastic water bottles and wondered if she was developing OCD. Next she checked the deadbolt on her front door...again. All of her windows were locked and boarded over from the inside so that no one could break the glass and get in.

She could hear sounds from outside the door. The doorknob rattled and she froze, not breathing. But then all was silent as whoever was on her porch moved on. She let out her breath, knowing that the deadbolt was secure.

Water, the universal solvent. So many things could dissolve in it.

Ashley remembered the first time she ever heard of hydrolysis of amides, occurring when nucleophile attacks carbon in the polar molecules of water. In acids, the carbonyl group becomes protonated, and this leads to a much easier nucleophilic attack. A terrorist group had added these acids to key water sources, setting off a chain reaction until it all became tainted.

Of course, at the time, she didn't understand what it meant. When she heard about the events on television, she wondered if the newscaster was saying there was a nuclear attack. It might as well have been, given the results throughout the world.

Because now, water was undrinkable. The source of life had been altered, and it was now a source of death. To drink the new water was to die, but to not drink any water was also to die.

All she had left of pure water from before the event was in her kitchen cabinet...how many bottles left? She checked again. Two.

She sat alone in her living room, the lamp her only illumination. She needed to think. Two plastic bottles of water would only last...three or four days. Then what? She had already taken all of the water out of the toilet and drank it. There was no other place in her house to find untainted water. Anything new coming out of the faucet was poison.

So her options were...either to stay here and die of thirst, or to leave her house, and go hunting for water...*out there.* Just like those who came onto her porch and rattled her doorknob.

***

The last bottle of water was drunk three days ago. Ashley had even tried to drink her own urine, but gagged so badly that she spat it out.

It was time to hunt.

She checked the clock on the mantle, the only source to reveal if it were night or day, since her windows were boarded up and covered so securely. Midnight. That meant it would be cooler outside, helping to expend less sweat. It was now or never.

She wore loose-fitting black clothes, including cargo pants with lots of pockets. In one of the pockets was a sharp knife. She knew she was desperate enough to use it on another person if it came to that.

Her hand touched the knob of the front door. Hesitating, remembering all the times it had been rattled by thirsty strangers who tried to get inside her house and couldn't, she finally reached for the deadbolt and turned it.

The door opened. A welcome breeze wafted over her, and she felt hope. It just seemed so normal...*so before.*

Stealthily she crept through her front yard, staying close to the fence, using it as cover. She kept her mouth open so that she could hear well. She moved slowly, stopping every two steps to listen, and then when she heard nothing, she continued on another two steps.

Quietly Ashley mounted the fence, held onto it on the other side, and let herself down gently. There would be no raucous jumping over the fence tonight. Everything must be as silent as the grave.

The sky was incredibly clear, and the moon was a tiny crescent. Once on the street, she picked up the pace, trotting on the sidewalk and staying close to dark shrubs and fences for their minimal aid of concealment.

She would not go to any grocery store; she understood that everyone else would have already raided those. Instead, she knew of another place...and hoped no one else had found it.

She traveled a few streets until she reached the locked cemetery gate and climbed over it. When her shoes touched the ground, the grass crunched and snapped...dry and dead like the bodies buried beneath it.

The entire cemetery was bent with age, as gravity pulled tree limbs towards the earth, and many headstones lay prone on the ground, victims of time and vandalism. But Ashley was not interested in the graves.

31

She found the mausoleum and went to the door. She knew that the lock was broken but that it did not appear broken from the outside. The thick door looked to any passersby as though it were secure and strong.

Now she would learn the verdict: was the fountain inside still working? The water that pumped through the fountain's plumbing held pure pre-nucleophilic water, recirculated over and over again from the pipe into the basin and back into the pipe, creating a pottery waterfall. Ashley had always wondered why such an ornament would be placed inside the mausoleum where no one would see it. But it didn't matter, the constant circulation of the water had surely kept it from stagnating and growing bacteria.

Quietly she removed the broken lock. She cringed as the heavy metal door creaked like something out of a haunted house when it opened. Musty air assaulted her nostrils from inside the mausoleum, but her knees went weak when she heard the sound of flowing water.

She entered the old crypt and closed the door behind her. She needed to protect her find, to be sure that no one would know there was pure water here. She reached into a pocket of her cargo pants and retrieved a flashlight.

Suddenly the flashlight was knocked from her hand. Ashley could hear it bounce and tumble onto the mausoleum's marble floor. She couldn't suppress a scream as she tried to scramble after the light. She felt strong hands grab her shoulders and she found herself pinned forcefully to the stone wall.

It was too dark to see, but she could smell sweat. She could hear the man's breathing as he suddenly let her go.

Trembling, revved up by adrenalin, Ashley reached into another pocket and grasped her knife. She pulled it quickly to arm level and thrust it towards the sounds of the breathing. Her knife made contact and she plunged it into yielding flesh as deeply as she could.

She heard him cry out and she could hear his body drop. She crawled across the marble floor, searching for her flashlight, found it and turned it on.

Shining the light on the man, she saw him lying prone, knife protruding from his chest and blood gushing onto the floor.

"I wasn't going to hurt you," he gasped. "I didn't mean to make you drop your flashlight."

"I won't share the water in here," Ashley said. She hated the sound of it; she was never a cruel person when water was plentiful, and she certainly had never hurt anyone. But now water was the most precious thing on earth, and she understood Darwin's mantra of the survival of the fittest. And here, a knife had made her the fittest.

"We don't have to share the water in this mausoleum," the man told her, his voice trembling with pain. "I know where there is more water, good water, enough for both of us…" his voice trailed off.

"Where?" Ashley asked eagerly, but the man slipped into unconsciousness. Remorse filled her, or was it perhaps, only regret? A few minutes later, he was dead, taking his secret with him.

She stood up and drank deeply from the fountain. It would do for now. And soon, she would be forced to hunt again.

10. INDIAN CARPET
Chris Reed

When Curtis Banks knocked on the door of 301 Orchard Creek Apartments, he didn't expect it to be answered by a giant Indian. Technically, the resident of the apartment was a Native American, but 'Indian' was the first word that popped into Curtis' mind. And the Indian was huge. He filled the entire doorway except for a small space over each shoulder through which Curtis could see the spinning blades of a dusty ceiling fan to the right, and the feathers of a headdress displayed upon the wall to the left.

"You the carpet guy?" the Indian asked, looking down on Curtis as if trying to decide whether he should let him in or squash him like a spider.

"Yeah," Curtis said nervously. He had never seen a man of such proportions, not even in prison.

The Indian shifted his massive bulk to the side and said, "Come on in."

Curtis grabbed the box containing his Windmaster 3000, kicked off his shoes, and went inside. The place was a veritable museum of Indian artifacts. Tomahawks and spears adorned the walls, along with animal skins, and cedar masks. There were portraits of others who bore a resemblance to the enormous resident, whom Curtis assumed to be his relatives. But who knew? They all looked alike to him.

He quickly averted his eyes toward the carpet so the Indian wouldn't catch him gawking at the potentially valuable items, in case he decided to pocket something before leaving. Curtis had initially thought that his five years in the joint had cured him of stealing, but kleptomania's not something that can be conquered quite that easily. It gets in the blood.

Also he preferred in general to avoid conversation with the residents. The last thing he needed was to get into a long, boring conversation about the Indian's ancestors trading buffalo skins to the white man for toilet paper or some crap. As far as Curtis was concerned, Indians were savages who had no business living among civilized people. They should be out on the range in their teepees instead of getting hand-outs from the government while people like him slaved over filthy, germ-infested carpets for a living.

Carpet like the Indian's. The dingy brown rug was stiff as broom bristles beneath his stocking feet.

"I want you to clean the living room and the dining room," the Indian told him.

"But the coupon's good for three rooms," Curtis said. "Don't you have a bedroom?"

"Not the bedroom," the Indian said, looking down on Curtis with eyes that seemed to project a stoic finality of the topic. "Just the living room and the dining room. Don't touch the bedroom door."

"Whatever," Curtis mumbled.

The Indian removed a floppy leather hat from a hat rack by the door and placed it atop his head. "I have to run a few errands," he said. "You can go ahead and get started. I won't be gone very long."

The Indian closed the door behind him as Curtis went to work assembling the vacuum's attachments. He cleaned the living room carpet, watching as the chunks of dirt flew into the transparent canister and swirled like a sandstorm. The dingy rug may have been a formidable challenge for an ordinary sweeper, but for the Windmaster and its 3000 G's of suck power, it was just another day at the office.

Curtis finished the living room, then guided the vac into the dining area. Debris crackled through the intake like gunfire, and when the room was done, the canister was teeming with a mass of black soot.

Curtis turned the Windmaster off and was about to begin the dismantling process when he spotted the Indian's bedroom door. It was open a little, just wide enough to look inside. Curtis put his eye up to the opening, but it was too dark in there to see anything. He pushed the door open a little more and let the light from the dining room filter in.

The room was decorated with more of the same, except hanging on the wall above the dresser was a large, black tapestry that read: WALK ABOVE THINE ENEMY SO THAT YE MAY TRAMPLE HIS SOUL.

"Weird," Curtis whispered.

The carpet in here was soft and fluffy beneath his feet. That was weird, too, considering the quality of the rest of the rugs he'd just cleaned. And such a variety of textures and colors… The whole room made him feel peculiar. It was almost as if…

He wouldn't let his mind complete the thought. He felt like a big pussy for even entertaining such a notion. But it wouldn't go away, it was all around him. It brought back a memory of when he was in prison, when that dude got shanked out on the weight pile, and how after he died you could still feel his presence there for weeks. Like the place was haunted. That's how the Indian's bedroom made him feel, like

35

something terrible had happened in there. The sensation was unmistakable.

"Probably just the germs in the air," Curtis said aloud, trying to calm his nerves. "It just needs a good cleaning."

He switched on the Windmaster and tried to push it, but the wheels were jammed. Something had wedged itself inside the inlet. He shut the vacuum off, then kneeled down and tilted it backward, feeling around underneath. There was a swatch of carpet stuck there that the Windmaster had ripped clean from the floor.

The bedroom light flashed on and Curtis looked up to find the Indian standing in the doorway. "Nineteen eighty-seven," the Indian said. "I caught him trying to steal my car stereo."

Curtis looked at the section of carpet he'd pried free of the vacuum. Soft. Fluffy. Blonde. At first, Curtis thought it was a toupee, until then noticed the bits of dried flesh that were attached.

"But he learned real quick," the Indian continued, "that you don't steal from the Shoshone. Nor do you trespass where you are not wanted."

Curtis dropped the clump of hair and backed away, looking around him at the checkerboard of blonde and brunette patches, suddenly realizing that he was sitting on a floor that was carpeted with human scalps.

The Indian stepped into the room. He had a tomahawk in his hand.

"I'm-I'm sorry," Curtis stammered. "I can fix it!"

"Don't worry," the Indian said as he reached for Curtis' head. "They're easy to replace."

11. THE CHASE
K. Trap Jones

They can run all they want; they're not going to get very far. Hell, I've lived on this land for my entire life and even I get turned around sometimes. It's the terrain that will do them in. The thick mud and heavy brush is a bitch to tread through. I remember one time, I was giving chase to one of my prey and I took a wrong step; damn near submerged myself within one of those hidden sinkholes. It took me about twenty minutes to climb out of that ditch. I ruined a perfectly good shotgun by having to stake it in the ground like that. I just couldn't get the mud out of the barrel; it was too far in there. I thought maybe firing the gun would dislodge the muck, but all that did was scar up my arm and shoulder when the damn thing exploded.

It's all about the chase. The prey should be given a head start; it's the polite thing to do down here in the south. Without the chase, it just doesn't seem like a worthy enough game to play. Now, don't get me wrong, I believe in a fair game. I'm not one to skip corners or cheat at the rules. Everything should be on a level playing field. The rules are simple, get across the creek and I let them go. It's not hard to understand, but getting to the creek is a real pain in the ass with all of the traps that I've set throughout the years, some of which I have no idea where they are. Last year, I fell into one of my ditches. It wasn't the fall that was the problem; it was the sharpened stakes at the bottom that really messed up my legs. I still have a small limp, but nothing that would stop the game from continuing.

I enjoy the thrill of the chase; the bond that is created like a spark to a dried leaf. I consider those that I hunt to be my friends. No other place in the world, would my visitors be able to interact with nature in the way that they do. I not only offer them that relationship, but I also give them a crash course in survival tactics. The best part about it all is that I do all of this for free. They come as they are and if they are successful, they leave much like they arrived.

Another aspect that I truly enjoy is the selection process of the weapons. I find that each hunt is completely different depending on the choice of weapon. The knives require close contact whereas the rifles can be from quite a long distance. Some require a lot more skill like the bow and arrow. Over the years, I found it very difficult to properly lead the arrow against a running person, so I will usually bring along a backup weapon if the bow fails me.

Like I said, the land is littered with traps, but I also have a few triggering items that help me locate the general direction of the prey. Trip wires with bells are the most common. The quick ring reassures me that I am indeed headed in the right direction. Another useful item is wind chimes. I never would have thought it, but I was surprised about how many of them actually run into them. In all of the confusion and panic, it must be frightening to accidentally trigger one of those location devices while knowing that I am listening.

Right now, I have two runners desperately trying to reach the creek. I always make sure that everyone knows the rules, but most choose to cry and whine instead of listening. I ignore their screams of agony and recite the rules like I always do. It is their choice whether to listen or not. But the one part that really gets me upset is that no one ever runs when I am done reading and the game has officially begun. They just stand there in disbelief or denial. A few bullets in the air usually prompt them back to reality, but still, I shouldn't have to waste the ammo.

The moment of choosing the weapon is always my favorite. Cleaned the night before, the weapons glisten in the rays of the southern sun; each desiring to be selected. My hand hovers over the machete and continues to the crossbow. My eyes scour the mace and survey the holstered pistols, but it is the chainsaw that shines the most brightly today. Freshly oiled with a brand new chain, the saw gleams with vengeance. The smell of the gas as it funnels into the weapon intoxicates me. The gurgling of the exhaust as I tighten the choke and the kickback of the power within the handle widens my eyes. With my prey on a head start, and the decision of weapon made, it's time to play.

12. THE MICROWAVE TOWER
Julianne Snow

I must have passed the same tower every day for the last thirty years. It stood so tall and yet, it blended so seamlessly into the background. I knew it was there, but it didn't register as anything other than part of the scenic backdrop of my focused world. That was until the day it all changed...

Have you ever wondered how technology really works? Up until that day, I had taken it for granted. Sure, I had a working knowledge of airwaves, sound waves, and even microwaves, but did I really understand what each of them actually entailed?

The answer to that question is a resounding no. As it turned out, the government experts had no idea how their new tower worked either.

It was a Friday. I remember the day clearly; it was one of only a few times that I had taken a different route to work. I hesitate to think of what would have happened had I not taken that right turn when I did...

I made it to work, a little later than usual, but I was still early. I liked that; having the time to grab a coffee from the tiny kiosk in the lobby before my busy day began. Nothing like a quiet moment to yourself to clear and refocus your head after the grind of traffic. It was at the kiosk that I first heard what had happened.

It's odd, you know. Hearing the news for the first time. I still find it hard to believe and if I hadn't seen them with my own eyes, I may not have ever truly believed it.

You're probably wondering what happened and to be honest, I'd love to tell you. The fact of the matter is that I don't know what happened. Well that's not entirely true; I know what happened, but I don't know *why* it happened. No one knows why.

The only thing we do know is that it was the experimental government tower, or microwave tower as it became known.

At 7:23am, the microwave tower sent out a signal or pulse or something that reached outward in a five kilometer radius around the circumference of its base. Anything within that radius, simply stopped.

They stopped, but they didn't stop living. They just stopped moving. Everyone and everything froze in the exact space that it had been occupying at the moment of the event.

The vehicles. The vegetation. The people. All stuck in stasis.

At first, emergency responders were afraid to enter the circle, but after their first tentative steps inside the ring, nothing had happened to them. They tried to render aid to those who were affected, but there was no helping them.

While technically not dead, they were certainly not alive either. The site has terrified some; so much so that the government attempted to cover them. You see it was impossible to move them; the pulse fused them permanently with the environment, as though everything within the circumference was now partially within our dimension and partially in another...

I remember the first time I passed the circle after it happened. The eerie feeling of utter stillness washed over me and for a moment, as the world around me slowed I was sure it had happened again. My throat filled with my fear and I vomited onto the steering wheel of my car. Once the moment had passed and I was dropped back into a world full of movement, waves of relief intermingled with disgust consumed me.

Many months elapsed before I even had the nerve to drive by again. My heart still exploded into my throat and my stomach crinkled itself into knots; my breakfast, thankfully, stayed on the inside this time.

After several years I was finally able to approach the ring without the security of my car surrounding me. By that time I was an old man, ancient by the standards of my grandchildren. The rest of the metropolis lived and churned callously around the stagnant circle as though it were not there. I knew why I felt compelled to search out those who had stopped that day, their souls and actions frozen in time, but that didn't stop me from feeling the fear.

I stood just outside the barrier that had been erected around the ring. It wasn't the type of obstacle that would stand in your way; it was more of a demarcation for people to comprehend that passing into the inner ring could have disastrous effects should anything of which they still did not comprehend, suddenly change.

Even as I fought the urge to turn away, my body propelled me forward, through the fence and into the living memorial. In silence, it waited. For what, I cannot say with any certainty. The overwhelming emotions of despair and loneliness played along my nerves like a song of pain and nostalgia. It was a heady phenomenon, this mix of emotions that resonated deep into my soul.

As I walked along the sidewalk, I studied the statuesque people as I passed them by. Men, women, and children caught unaware in mid step, in mid swallow, in mid call. If you haven't seen inside of the circle yet, picture the busiest moment on the street that you can remember and capture it for an instant, as if you've taken a photograph. That's the best way to describe it; a photographic moment etched into life-sized stone relief. Every detail down to the last wisp of hair blown awry by an errant gust, petrified against the backdrop of the elements.

When I had found her, my heart broke anew. After returning home that fateful day so many years ago, I had searched the house for her, hoping that she had not made it to work before the pulse had struck. My cell phone pleas had all gone unanswered and deep down I knew what that meant, despite my denial. The empty house was the proof I received.

The second piece of corroborating evidence came in the form of two FBI Special Agents about three months after the event. I had reported my wife as missing and potentially within the circumference as the authorities had instructed us to do in the days following the pulse. My heart was heavy making that call, but what else could I have done? I wanted the answer even though I knew it would hurt to hear it. I knew what the truth was, but I still wanted to see for myself.

That was why I entered the ring at last, after all of these years. It had taken me that long to build the nerve to do so, the nerve to see Catherine again.

When I found her, it was as though no time had passed for her. She had been caught in mid stride, her left hand searching the expanse of her purse for some object. She looked as if she might topple, but strangely, her body was balanced on the ball of her right foot. By the laws of physics, there was no way that she should have remained upright, but the pulse had suspended them. I stood for a long time, my eyes gazing upon her beautiful face and my heart breaking because I knew that deep inside, her body still lived. Scientists who studied the phenomenon had recently let it be known that while time had essentially stopped for those caught up in the pulse, their life force had not.

Life. It's such a funny word. Those poor people were not living by the standards that you and I would define, but they were alive. Alive. Such a sad word when taken into context sometimes.

Placing one last kiss upon her face, I left the circle from the direction I had entered; dreading the coming months of loneliness as I contemplated my own death. Even in death, we would not be reunited and that was a hard truth to accept.

***

And so the circle around the tower remains; a silenced and macabre garden of statuaries that stand in effigy of what can happen, of what did happen.

One thing is for certain; people no longer live within five kilometers of any mechanized government towers. Anywhere. The lesson has not been forgotten, and a wariness of technology born from that moment. A moment that froze time and space in the oddest of ways, creating mourners of those yet living…

13. CORPUS DELECTABLE
Sydney Leigh

"Eat me," I whispered into your ear.

Your lips gently traced the sloping curves of my neck as I pressed into your body upon the warmth of our bed.

"Do you really want me to?" you asked breathlessly, between kisses.

"Yes," I answered desperately. *"Please. I need you to."*

Your mouth found mine for one passionate moment before you backed down and your face disappeared into the darkness under the sheets.

As I moaned, I felt the gravel of your words against my skin. *I love you*, they said.

"I love you, too," I answered back, and closed my eyes.

***

When I woke from the dream, your oversized t-shirt clung to the perspiration pooled in the swale of my chest, I noticed the blue glow of the computer screen stealing out under the door to your office.

I must still be dreaming, I thought. You'd been dead for a year now.

Sometimes, in the shadowy dread of inveterate nightmares, I'd roll over in bed and you'd be there, your back to me, the back of your head splayed open from the bullet and soaking the chambray sheets with shards of flesh and blood. In others, I'd close the mirrored door of the medicine cabinet after swallowing a mouthful of Prozac, and you'd be looking back at me; the smoke from the gun floating from your open mouth like you'd just taken a drag from a cigarette and didn't inhale.

But this was no dream.

I pushed open the door slowly, two prayers silently vying across my lips. In one, I yearned for you to be there, an invocation that your death itself was the dream--that waking now, I'd find you just as you'd been that night, before closing your lips around the cold steel of the handgun's barrel.

And one begged mercilessly that you would not.

But there you were, your silhouette illuminated dimly by the screen, your hands resting beside you on the arms of your executive leather chair. The smell of sulfur from the gunshot suspended in the small room grew sweet in comparison to what I knew could only be the senescence of you.

Stepping closer, my insides pitching from the efflux, I saw you turn slightly at my presence. My bare feet seemed to fuse with the taut carpet under me as I discerned the grossly flawed contour of the back of your head. The chair swiveled slowly, deliberately, as your anchored feet brought us face to *almost* face.

Your malachite skin hung in sallow, fleshy strips, your eyes grievously displaced amidst the once perfect symmetry of your features. Your smile revealed a black chasm from which tiny, legless creatures crawled, writhing luridly along the gangrenous points of your teeth.

I reeled and stumbled backwards, awakening with my back pressed against the wooden threshold of the doorway. You lowered yourself down as the words echoed deafeningly inside my head.

Eat me, I heard myself say, and felt the blessed agony of your first bite.

14. LAST WORDS
S.C. Hayden

It was important not to let them grandstand. A few words were all you could give them. It was dignified to give them that, but you couldn't let them take over the show, cause they'd turn the place into a three-ring circus just as quick as they pleased.

The best was something simple like: "I want the victim's family to know I'm sorry." or "I want my family to know I love them." Something like that was best. Something that made everyone feel better. Even if their last words were something like: "I never did it, I swear. I never killt em." Even that was okay so long as it was short. Just so long as you didn't let it go on for too long.

There were people there watching them and they knew it. Often, the victim's close friends and family, someone from the paper, sometimes even the Governor was there. That's why you couldn't let them grandstand. If you gave them a chance to make a show, they'd take it.

Sometimes they just got scared. They got so scared that their legs went out from underneath them, and I understood that. I had nothing against those folks. The guards were trained for that sort of thing. We'd hold the fella up by his arms so he didn't fall and someone would place the hood over his head and tighten the noose around his neck and we wouldn't ask him if he wanted to say anything because he was too scared and there was no point. I had nothing against a fella who got too scared.

Some folks though, some fellas figured they'd rather go out in a blaze of glory. Some would act real calm, like they were resigned to their fate. They'd look the priest in the eye and say: "Pray for me father." and when they were asked if they had any last words, they'd let out a whoop and holler and see if they couldn't knock a guard or two off of the tower, yelling: "Look at me Governor! Whoooeee! I bet you never seen one like me before."

Those folks never surprised me though. I could always feel it. I would watch their eyes and I could tell. When they were asked if they had any last words, I would look at the muscles in their neck and when I saw them tense up, I got my club ready because I knew what was coming.

When we hanged John Haggerty, I did not expect it to happen the way it did. John Haggerty stood on the platform, hands shackled behind his back, eyes shining like silver dollars, and smiled. When we asked him if he had any last words, he puffed out his chest and yelled: "Governor." Right then we tried to put the hood on him because we knew he was going to be trouble, but he started thrashing from side to side and turned out to be one hell of a lot stronger than he looked. "Governor," he shouted, "tell em bout little Jimmy Owens. Tell em what you did."

We brought the clubs down on the back of Haggerty's head just as hard as we could but it was like hitting an engine block. The Governor jumped up out of his seat and came rushing toward the tower, shouting: "I want that man hanged. I want that man hanged right now goddamn it."

We got the noose over Haggerty's head but we couldn't get it tight around his neck because he kept hunching up his powerful shoulders and swinging his head from side to side, shouting all the while: "Tell em what you did Governor. Tell em bout how you touched that little boy after his momma died. Tell em bout how you sent that boy to a mental institution so's nobody would know about it." And all the while the Governor was shouting out: "I said I want that man hanged!"

I stepped in front of John Haggerty and forced the noose tight around his neck. That's when John Haggerty looked me in the eyes and said: "Who owns you boy? No one owns me. No one owns John Haggerty." And finally it was over. We all stepped away and someone tripped the latch and John Haggerty went down the chute.

I looked down the shoot at John swinging beneath us. He hung there, limp and lifeless; his eyes bulging out of his head and bleeding. We never did get the hood on him. Then I looked down at the Governor. He was panting and his hands were trembling. He looked like a man who'd just had a real scare.

That was the last time I ever participated in a hanging, and my last day working for the state of Mississippi. I don't know if John Haggerty was speaking fact or fiction, but whenever I hear the Governor's voice on the radio, I remember the way his hands were trembling and that look of fear in his eyes, and I hear John Haggerty's voice asking me: "Who owns you boy?"

15. IN THE LONDON FOG
Doug Robbins

Down in his basement laboratory Dr. Evans looked upon the reanimated corpse he had created. Its eyes were yellowed and its skin was the hue of putrid green. After all of these years of tinkering with the dead, he no longer noticed the smell.

The creature raised its hideous head and released an ugly groan. The doctor placed his hand on the creature's forehead and gazed into the corpse's rotting eyes. "I gave you life, now go and do my bidding child," the mad doctor whispered. The doctor unbound the creature's arms and legs and the abomination shambled out the front door and vanished into the London fog.

Nearby in the mist a gentleman walked with his son through the thick London air. Both the boy and the man carried presents under their arms. It was Christmas Eve and they had been purchasing last minute gifts.

"Will grandmamma and grandpapa be there when we arrive, father?" the boy asked.

"I would imagine so," said his father Francis, as the thick fog swirled about them and the visibility was obscured. He spoke through clenched teeth that held a pipe.

The boy was enveloped in the haze and momentarily vanished. Francis heard the boy scream but could not see where the youth had gone. "It's got me papa help me please!" the boy screamed as his wailing voice was carried off into the fog.

"What's got you Jonathan, where are you!" Francis yelled.

When he found him in the haze Francis dropped the presents upon the street. He cried out to the heavens when he saw his boy's twisted and mangled corpse lying face down upon the bricks. His clothes were torn and he was drenched in his own blood.

Francis' knees trembled and his stomach lurched. He was filled with sheer revulsion. He fell to his hands and knees and wretched the contents of his guts upon the curb. He wiped the spittle away from his lips and buried his face into his hands, weeping openly.

"My boy my boy, oh God, who murdered my poor boy!" he sobbed.

The reanimated corpse shambled out of the darkness and Francis covered his mouth aghast.

"Good lord!" he shrieked.

Francis ran through the fog and into the nearest tavern screaming frantically. "My boy's been murdered by... by... a dead man!" he screamed.

Some within the tavern gasped, and some produced nervous, drunken laughter. "Hey this wanker thinks there's a zombie loose on the streets of London," one of the patrons joked.

The door swung open and the creature shambled inside in pursuit of its elusive prey. The patrons screamed and shrieked as they ran toward the rear door. The corpse's yellow eyes fixed themselves on Francis, as the bartender pulled out a pistol and shot the abomination multiple times in the chest and then the head. The creature's chest was perforated and its rotten brains dripped through the gaping hole that had appeared in the middle of its forehead. But onward it strode.

The corpse shuffled toward the bartender as he emptied the remaining rounds into the zombie's skull. When the gun was empty, the walking corpse overtook him, both strangling and frightening the bartender to death, with strength that was somehow present within its rotting hands.

Francis fled outside into the dense air of the fog, feeling certain that the zombie pursued him. He shrieked and ran into the haze of the night, not once looking behind him. He ran until his lungs wheezed and he could run no more, collapsing amidst a gathering of garbage cans and boxes. He peered out between them, watching the London fog condense, and then close the trail which he had just moments before, pushed through it. Somewhere out in that blinding white mist walked the rotting flesh that had killed his boy.

16. WORLDS COLLIDE AND THEN SEPARATE
Vince Liberato

I threw the punch as hard as I could. My arm, the only arm on our shared body that I control, barely reaches past the spot where our flesh is fused. Its target, a mirror image of myself, even has an eye patch (but on the opposite eye), blocks and strikes back, just as feebly. Our hands slap at each other and our feet kick off in random, spasmodic angles. The world around me looks like something out of a Picasso, with several tables sporting new angles, double-sided test tubes, chairs that appear to be made of nothing but legs, and my poor cat, now joined to an identical tabby at the legs, is fighting itself with even less success than I am. The poor thing now looks as if somebody purposely put a cat-shaped paint splatter on a Rorschach test before folding the paper. The handful of other researchers I worked with fared even worse. One had been joined at the face and had suffocated with no mouth or nose to breath. Another had seemingly been merged at the heart by a thin line of muscle and flesh. She tore it in half when she and her counterpart pulled away from each other in a very King Solomon-esque resolution over its ownership. The Window is the least changed thing in the room and both the cause and solution to the problem at hand, which, unlike the rest of my now-conjoined world, looks almost indistinguishable to how it did fifteen minutes ago. It only grew an extra lever.

Why I (and my counterpart) built our respective Windows, why it malfunctioned, and why when two parallel worlds violently crash together, all of creation is partially merged with its other universe's counterpart are not the issues at hand. My biggest concern since this nightmarish vaudeville act started are the two levers - a green lever and a red lever, one from my dimension and one from his, both now a part of the same machine. When one is pulled, it will reverse the process and detach our two fused dimensions. When the other is pulled, the same. Unfortunately, due to the nature of the merger, it seems that neither one of us can afford to let the other get to their respective lever. When worlds collide and then separate, there is no way for things to be corrected without a bit of a mess, and this, like all separations, splitting up will come with a very high price. Think of it like a divorce, only with the merged flesh of the shared body going to the victor and the loser reduced to a bloody pile of whatever remained.

I throw another weak punch. He caught it, gripping my hand tightly this time. By the look on his face - my face - I could tell he was tired of our fight. I was too.

"We should talk this out," he said.

I nodded, but kept my guard up. I quickly scanned the room for weapons. All I could see were double-headed pens resting on the monitor.

"I don't want to kill your universe, but I don't want you to kill mine." He continued his proposal. "It seems like we are surviving just fine like this. I am not in pain and I don't think you are. You and I…We can work together. Find a way to reverse this, but without ripping billions to pieces. Thousands, if not millions may have already died because of us."

I gestured towards one of the television monitors with one hand and picked up one of the pens resting in his blind spot. They were no longer smooth flat screens, but tetrahedrons stretched in odd angles that still somehow worked when turned on. On the screen, the chaos and destruction was much worse than I could have imagined. He and I, we were the lucky ones. If you asked a doctor, we could be classified as thoraco-omphalopagus conjoined twins. We were joined at the side and most likely shared a heart, some digestive organs, and part of a liver. The images we were seeing now were what could possibly be described as a freak show's parade of the conjoined on a world-wide scale. Some were merged at the skull, others the entirety of their chest or back. The most horrifying were the slowly dying men and women who found themselves attached to dead counterparts who had died in the opposite universe weeks or even months before. Sections of necrotic flesh were beautifully woven into the half-dead, turning a few unfortunates into a near literal human interpretation of Schrodinger's Cat. My double was mesmerized and kept his eye off of me.

"This is… What have I done?"

"You dropped your guard," I said, shoving a double-headed pen into his remaining eye. His arm and leg jutted out, hitting nothing. He died seconds later. I knew when. I could feel it.

Having a part of you die is an experience I would never want to relive. Our major shared organs slowed, but did not shut down completely. With my only working arm and only working leg, I drug myself to the Window and pulled *my* lever.

There was a blinding flash, a noise like two twisted pieces of metal being pulled apart, and suddenly I had two arms and two legs I could control. My lab looked the same as it had before. I felt as I had before, and my coworkers were all whole too, although understandably quite upset with me. The cat, clearly distressed also, stretched her legs and snaked off to find something else to fight, her twitching tail lingered in the doorframe before disappearing. On the display of television feeds, the dying and the suffering were back to normal, as was the rest of the world.

The pen was still in my hand, albeit with only a single pointed end. I wiped the blood off using my coat and started filling out the appropriate paperwork. I was sure to be hearing about this little debacle for weeks.

17. STAY
Devlin Giroux

Hated it when someone like her sat at my table. Friday, 6:30pm, and she sat. Check just cashed, no groceries yet, and she sat right down.

"Cashing three hundred."

The pit boss nodded. What did he care? I slammed three bills into the box. The woman took her chips, held them close, her precious pieces of plastic.

She played two hands, a 20-chip each. Clothes thin, hair filthy, crusted stain on her left shoulder.

King – six on the first hand. Called for a hit. Should have stayed. She pulled a ten and busts. Seven – six on the second. Another hit, drew a jack. Over that fast. Forty bucks gone and going strong. Sorry, Molly, or whatever the hell her kid's name was, but no food tonight, honey. Mommy had a bad night at the table. I'm sure you'll understand.

She wanted two more hands. Nailed an ace – jack. Thirty bucks for her. She took the chips, held them like jewels. I couldn't help but wonder when the last time was her child, or children, had felt that touch, that gaze, that worth. Her happiness didn't last. She lost the second by playing cocky on ten – seven. I turned over twin ladies. Net gain that round: a whole ten bucks. Sorry, honey, that bastard dealer was a cheat. I could have bought you new clothes if he wasn't such a bad man.

Fuck you, lady. I didn't want you at my table.

I tossed her four more cards. She split a seven – seven, played three-handed. Drew a ten on the first, king on the second. She wised up and stayed on both. Her alligator skin finger tapped red felt for the hit on a two – five. Another king winked up at her. Not bad with three seventeens, chances were good she'd take those hands. I flipped my hole card, a jack of diamonds dancing with my ebon lady. The stench from her open-mouthed sigh curled my nose hairs.

What do you want, lady? Should I feel sorry for you? I didn't put a damn gun to your head. You sat at my table.

Suit pulled up next to her. He smiled, all whites and brights. Something was wrong with him, but I couldn't figure it right away, seeing as I had too much hate on for Molly's Mom.

"Cashing five hundred."

Five more bills down the slot. I passed the man his chips, not looking too closely.

He dropped one for the woman's two. She lost both hands. He won, twenty-one against my nineteen. Nothing spectacular to his win, but he kept shining me with that damn smile. Man looked over to Molly's Mom and leaned close. He spoke a whisper. Still heard him, though.

"Time to leave, ma'am," he said.

"I'll leave when I'm damn good and ready," she shot back. I hated her, but had to give her a grin for the attitude. Yeah, fuck right off, buddy.

"Leave now or I'll go to your house, slit your husband's throat, and use his blood to slide in on Beth as she screams for you."

The smile never left his face as he said it. I'm no daisy, but those words…those words came from a deep darkness I'd sooner gargle with buckshot than feel inside me.

Molly's Mom stammered something, but she was gone in seconds, chips forgotten.

"Looks like I can take a break," I said.

That damn smile again. "Whatever do you mean? I have chips to play."

"Talk to someone like that at my table, you have to go. Make it hard for me and you get an escort on your way out the door."

"I won't be going anywhere until we speak, Mr. Montrosse," he said.

My turn to smile. "Had to be her. She would send someone like you to get my Hancock. Not happening. Take yourself and the papers back to that ragged slash and tell her she can stand in front of me her damn self and beg for that ink."

"I assure you it's nothing that mundane, Neil." He pushed all his chips aside.

"What's she paying you? Is there good money in strong arming?"

"I'm not here to force you into anything."

"Good to know." Was hard not to jump the table on him. That smile was razors on blue eyes. "Security or your own steam. Your call."

"See? Right there. That contempt. It's what caught our attention."

"Tell it walking," I said. I signaled the pit boss. "I promise I'll write."

I looked behind me, hoping to see Stu and Crew stomping my way. What I saw was the side of beef staring right through me. He had to have seen the gesture to 86 the suit, but he stood there with a thousand-yard stare, jaw slack.

"Stu Baxter recognizes a true predator, Mr. Montrosse," the suit said. Damn, the man was good at smug. He flicked a finger and Stu looked like he remembered something urgent needed doing someplace far from me. "I want to offer you a job. You've been scouted, and I think we can work well together."

"Already have one, unless you think fucking up mortgages is just a hobby of mine."

"Flipping cards and slinging chips, sure, but it wouldn't trouble you in the least if they all choked to death on their own bile right in front of you."

"Would love if you tossed a point in here somewhere, Freud."

I didn't think it possible, but that smile of his got wider and whiter.

"The name's Mr. Gone," he said, "and I want you to kill."

"Kill who?"

"Them all."

"I'm not a murderer," I said. Part of me even meant it. "Stand up and get to stepping."

"Is it murder when a hunter thins the herd, Mr. Montrosse?" He adjusted his tie, gaze canvassing the casino's crowd. "That's what we do. What you can do. Disease, disaster, or hands on. We won't interfere with your artistic or professional expression."

"And you need to be fitted for a straightjacket." I showed my hands for the cameras, both sides and fingers splayed, before giving Mr. Gone my back. "I'm going home."

No one said bye as I changed into my streets. If Stu minded the fact I was cutting out two hours early, he kept it to himself, seeing how he turned away as I walked past him on the way out the door.

"Think about the number of people who go missing in a single year, Mr. Montrosse," the suit said beside me, matching my stride. "Never seen again. Sure, some of them go missing because of your freelance sociopaths, as you do have some talented amateurs in your ranks, but they're all about ritual and badly disguised metaphors for sex."

I lit a Winston without breaking my gait.

"With that finely tuned contempt," he said, "I see you as the personal type. A strangler maybe. You want them to see you, want them looking into your eyes as the light leaves their own."

"Only one about to see the lights go out is you if you don't get the hell off my back, asshole."

He stopped and grabbed my shoulder, spinning me about face. Felt like frozen centipedes crawling down my soul, that touch of his. "The direct approach, then. Here you go, Mr. Montrosse. Have fun."

Nothing went black, no flash of light. I was just standing over a child asleep in her bed. The stink jumped up and slapped me across the face. Cheap and sweet to mask the sick. I was in the only place that made sense.

"Evening, Molly," I said. I was a lot of things in life, some of them even good and respectable, but never slow. "Sorry she brought this into your world. There'll be something better waiting for you after tonight."

The air behind me filled. Mr. Gone's smile slithered across my nerves.

"She can't hear you," he said.

"Good to know, Clarence." We left before being too close poisoned her dreams. She'd suffered enough, I was sure. We were in another bedroom in the time it takes a shadow to spread. It wasn't an unpleasant sensation.

"This is why you're here," Mr. Gone said. "Style is all up to you."

I toed an empty bottle aside. Black Velvet.

"The first is an easy one," he said. "We make it that way so our candidates don't suffer sentimentality."

"Then you did this one up right." I stared down at the stain. "She'll hear me?"

"If you want."

"Take a walk," I said. "Or whatever the hell it is you do."

It slipped from my sleeve. I caught it between my fingers as natural as a lie. Felt heavy, far too solid. Was only right, what with the years of discord and despair I'd sown with the turn of a card. Damn near laughed when I saw the painted face smiling back at me. That suicide king shined me as bright as Mr. Gone.

I stood over that woman, knowing what I wanted to do. Didn't feel right. Also didn't feel all that wrong.

18. HUNTED
Michael Schomaker

The wind is cool and brisk; it always is this time of year. It blows through the grass and makes it dance from side to side. The brown and orange leaves that are still left on the trees rattle so loudly that I can barely hear my footsteps on the crunchy forest floor. I've been hunting the forests of Michigan all of my life. It is the only place where I feel at home, alive like I was meant to be here.

As I meander through the woods, my destination is an old hunting blind, one of many that I visit from time to time. I try to not think about the outside world as I walk, for this is my world at the moment. The squirrels jumping from tree to tree hardly seem to notice me at all, covered from head to toe in camouflage. The crows caw in the distance - this is the music of the forest!

I am getting closer to my blind now, which is only a half hour walk from the road. But something begins to feel different this day. I've walked these woods hundreds of times before, but the odd feeling will not leave me. I start walking a little faster not exactly sure why – perhaps just anxious to hunt? *"Or is it something else?"* an inner voice whispers. I am unable to shake this feeling. The crows have quieted now. The squirrels have all but disappeared. *Maybe I'm making too much noise.* I attempt to laugh it off just to lighten my mood.

A large branch snaps in the distance. Now this happens all of the time but today it bothers me unusually. I stop walking for a minute to listen. *Was it a deer? Or was someone else in the forest with me this evening?* Surely it's nothing out of the ordinary, and I'll be at my blind in a minute.

There it is. I see my blind in the distance. See, phantom jitters, I mutter to myself. But as I walk toward it I swear I hear footsteps crunching along with my own. I stop again only a few yards further onward. Something sure seems different out here this afternoon. I hear something scurry across the forest floor. I immediately turn toward the sound and see nothing. I call out then, which I never do, "Hello anyone there?"

I wait a few seconds then start moving again, but with a bit more speed. Just as I reach the door of my hunting blind I see movement out of the corner of my eye. It was too tall to be any animal that I've seen in these woods. I panic a little, force open the door, and jump quickly inside. I slam it behind me and start peering through the small window holes that had been cut out of the wall years ago.

I'm breathing heavily now, and it's hard to catch my breath. I have been here a thousand times over and I feel foolish, but there is surely something different this time. I sit back and close my eyes, and relax for a few minutes to try and let the peculiar anxiety pass.

My rapid breathing begins to calm. I am slowly getting control of myself. I take another deep breath when something slams suddenly against the side of the old blind! I am literally jolted from the small chair I had been sitting in. I clasp my rifle tightly, pointing it at the door as if I expected someone to come barging through. My chest is heaving - hands trembling!

"What's going on!?" I yell blindly with fear. After a few minutes of silence and sitting on the damp wooden floor I rise up to peer again from the window. I see something. *What is it?* It's large, dark, and the body looks to be fully covered in fur. *Good lord it's big! Has to be 7 or 8 feet tall!*

It's just watching me, moving from tree to tree staring me down. My hands have stopped trembling now, probably from shear astonishment. *"But what exactly am I seeing here?"* I watch the creature for what seems like the better part of an hour. It crouches just far enough away from me that I am unable to discern any more detail. More time passes and it begins to slip slowly away into the distance, until I do not believe that I can see it any longer. As the forest floor darkens I realize that there are only about 30 minutes more of daylight before darkness falls.

This horrible realization jolts me anew with adrenaline and my mind spins as I ponder whether or not this unknown animal will let me leave. My nerves are shot and I decide that I will attempt to leave the blind. I open the door and look around, and the coast seems clear. One cautious step with my hairs standing on end, and then another. Then as I start to move a bit more quickly, I hear it. The creature is coming up now behind me. I bolt and run down my trail! Absolute panic has now set in.

I run through the woods and can only think of getting to the truck. Running frantically I hear my footfalls and my gasping, and I imagine it to be that of the beast. Running upon my heels and breathing down my neck!

Just about halfway now, and I know it is still behind me. Suddenly I trip, falling face first and sliding wildly into the leaves of the forest floor. *Pure terror!* I stay face in the dirt for mere moments with senses heightened, smelling the pungent earth.

When I can finally bring myself to my knees I see the creature not twenty yards away. I look into its eyes and see something I don't expect. I don't see a hungry animal that seeks the taste of my blood. I don't see an animal protecting its young. I see *emotion*, something deep and profound in its eyes. It stands motionless, brow furrowed, and seems to wait to see what I will do. And I see then something else in the creature's glare, a look of anger or possibly hatred. The creature wants me gone, and somehow I know that it will ensure this happens, one way or another.

I slowly rise to my feet, eyes never leaving the creature and his never leaving mine. It stands motionless, watching me as I shakily move toward the road. I can sense that it still follows me, but seems to back off as I near the tree line.

When I finally arrive at my truck I turn and the creature is gone, like it was never there in the first place. The entire ride home my befuddled mind swims as I try to interpret the events of the day. I never did understand with certainty what happened that cool fall evening. I have only since shared my story with a very select few, and now anonymously with anyone who reads this.

Believe what you will about this tale, but I do however have some advice for those who venture into the woodlands of Michigan. When you hear a branch break in the distance, or a pile of leaves rustle in the thick just behind you. This is *their* home, the flora and fauna of the forest, and how would you feel with uninvited guests in yours?

As for me, I no longer hunt anywhere near that stretch of forest. I tell my friends simply that there are no deer out there anymore. But now you know the real story.

19. HEADLIGHTS
Mark Slade

Sean rose from his bed, feeling the dampness of sweat on his arms. He rubbed the middle of his forehead with two fingers, yawned. Outside his bedroom window the sun was setting. In another three hours, he would make his way down Highway 20 to the warehouse and work another twelve hour shift boxing up assorted chocolates and placing them on a pallet. Cora was in the other room playing on the computer. He could see the light from the monitor flicker in the dark room across the hallway.

He threw on a pair of jeans and a sweater, and clumsily staggered to the other bedroom. He saw Cora staring intently at the screen, her large framed glasses sitting at the end of her nose. He waited by the doorway, and then decided not to disturb her. He wanted to sit with her, but she had just finished work at the dry cleaners an hour before and he was sure she needed some time to unwind.

Sean went to the kitchen, looked in the refrigerator, and grabbed a handful of ham and shoved the sliced meat into his mouth. He reached for the gallon of milk, when some headlights coming down the lane caught his attention. It was blindingly bright, passing through the kitchen window. Sean squinted, raised his arm to block the light from his eyes.

He went to the backdoor, opened it slightly, and peeked out. No one was there. The headlights were gone. No car out in his driveway. He and Cora lived a good two miles from the next neighbor, so it was a big deal when someone drove up to his house after dark. In the past year, only Cora's Dad had visited and maybe Jones from work. Since all ties were broken with Sean's family, and it would take more than an episode of Oprah to sort it all out, chances of a visitor out of the blue, were rare.

Sean shrugged and closed the door. "Strange," He said to himself. "Maybe I'm still dreaming." He poured himself a glass of milk, took a long sip. Then he placed the glass on the table and went to the room where Cora was still watching YouTube on the computer.

Sean leaned against the doorway. "Hey," He said, his voice booming.

It took a second before Cora realized he had said something. She removed the headphone from her tangled brown hair, smiled. "You said something?"

Sean nodded. "How was your day?"

"Okay. Didn't know you were up." Cora swirled around in her swivel chair.

"Been up a few minutes. Did you see the headlights coming down the lane?"

Sean rubbed the sleep out of his eyes.

"No. Who's here?" Cora folded her arms, stretched her neck to see out the window.

"That's the weird thing. Nobody is here. I saw the headlights, almost blinded me. I poked my head out the backdoor, no car there." Sean shrugged and laughed.

"I bet you were dreaming or something." Cora stood. She walked up to Sean and kissed him.

"That's what I thought too. But....I don't know."

Cora patted him on the stomach. "I'll go make you some eggs. How's that?"

"Yeah... okay." Sean said. He stepped aside and let her past him. He followed her to the kitchen.

Sean rose from his bed, feeling the dampness of sweat on his arms. He rubbed the middle of his forehead with two fingers, yawned. Outside his bedroom window the sun was just finishing the process of setting. He saw the headlights coming down the lane. He slid on a pair of jeans and a shirt. He ran through the hall and into the kitchen. He opened the backdoor and stepped out on the cold ground. Cora put the Metro in park and turned off the engine. She quickly got out of the car, and left the driver's door wide open. She was sobbing, and trying to talk on her cell phone. She stumbled through the yard and walked through Sean, and into the house.

Sean heard her say through the tears, "Dad....Sean...Sean was killed this morning....another car....."

Sean followed her in, and became a memory…

20. SABBATICAL IN THE OHIO METHLANDS
Joe McKinney

Not *really* zombies.

Not like in the movies, anyway. To begin with, they're alive. And they don't eat their victims. They'll rape you, rob you, murder you, sure, but not eat you.

The rest of it's the same, though.

They lurch around looking dead. They smell dead. Boils; abscesses; old infected injuries; they all do their part in approximating putrefaction. Sometimes, a murmuring haze of flies will surround their eyes and mouths. They look like skeletons in leather sheets. Their knee joints have a bigger circumference than their thighs. Starvation and malnutrition are the norm. But their crippled movements and disoriented moaning can be deceptive. Step into the street with your head elsewhere and they'll swarm you.

Afterwards, your corpse will look like it's been eaten.

But they don't eat you.

Just...tear you up.

I've seen it happen too many times. Some family in a station wagon, just passing through, gets lost, doesn't see the roadblocks. College kids looking for a gag. Survivalists, testing their mettle, and failing. I even watched them get an Ohio state trooper once. But usually those guys know better.

This is the sixth year I've been coming to what used to be Gatling, Ohio. Like most of the small towns in America's midsection, Gatling was abandoned after the Meth Rebellion of 2019, given over to the meth zombies who now wander its streets and sleep in the doorways of its uninspired, post-WWII architecture. The buildings are falling apart. Few of the windows remain unbroken. Insulation hangs from the ceilings. Scrolls of wallpaper curl off the walls. The only life here is that which feeds off meth and wanders the streets, moaning like something out of a Romero film, looking for the high that will take them through the coming night.

Luckily, the little second floor dentist office I've taken over as my observation point has escaped the depravations. During the day, when the meth zombies are most active, I can sit at the window and get film footage or dictate notes, whatever I feel like doing. At night, I sit in the old patient's chair and read Jack Finney novels and drink gin. It's diligent field work - don't get me wrong - but I enjoy my summers here in Gatling just the same.

Gene Northrop, a chemistry professor from Texas A&M, has a similar setup across town in the old New Life Baptist church. I've seen him around some. He's working on a paper on aboriginal techniques for methamphetamine production in the post-industrial ruins of abandoned America. Sometimes, late at night, I'll hear a building explode at the edge of town, and I think to myself, *Ah, one of Gene's grad students just scored himself a paper.* Some night soon I'm going to visit him. Maybe we can compare notes.

In the meantime, I've been working on a paper on the mating habits of the female meth –

***

Okay, I need to change gears for a second.

There was a noise outside the door just a bit ago and I had to make sure it wasn't a wrecking party. The males can be dangerous when they're scavenging for a high. I had to shoot a few of them earlier this month. I hated doing it, but I have to preserve this observation post.

Luckily, it was only Susan.

She started coming here, to my office, two years ago. She's a white female, early 20s, which means that she was probably still in her teens when the Rebellion happened. The meth has charred most of her mind to cinders, but her survival instincts are still strong.

She caught me off guard the first time she came here. It was late at night. I had gone through a lot of gin. I got up from my dentist's chair to jot down some notes on something I'd seen that day, forgetting the front door was still unlocked. I heard a floorboard creak and turned around. She was squatting in the middle of the floor, dressed in rags, her long brown hair a frizzled, shaggy mass around her dirty face, nicks and cuts all over her hands and arms.

Have you ever been watched by a squirrel? Same nervous, unblinking look I got from her.

I tried to speak, but she scrambled toward the door. She didn't make it far, though. She was hungry, dehydrated, her body weak.

I gave her some clean water and let her sleep on my couch. When she woke the next morning, she was going through withdrawal. She looked at the clean clothes I'd dressed her in, touched her face that I'd scrubbed clean, and panicked. *Residual feelings of violation?* I

62

wondered. I watched her from my desk. I put a military MRE on the floor. She snatched it up and backed toward the open door. I didn't make a move to stop her, just went on smiling.

I was delighted when she came back the next night.

We developed a routine. I'd leave the door cracked at night, a little food and water on the chair next to my bed. Though she never talked, she could still communicate, with her eyes and her body language.

She seemed grateful. I know I was.

I started calling her Susan, after this girl I used to dream of dating back in my grad school days. I don't think my meth girl minded. It seemed to comfort to her, just as she became a comfort to me. She became my bulwark against the loneliness that used to overwhelm me here at night in the Methlands.

I've been back in Gatling for three days now. That first night, when I was still getting settled, she came to me. She had something to show me, a memento of our last night together last August.

Now I'm sitting here at my desk, watching her rub her belly, and I can't help but wonder if her baby will be born without a soul, or if it will lose it along the way.

Like its father.

21. CHRISTMAS NIGHT
Christopher Conlon
Originally published in *Festive Fear: Global Edition*

One quiet night a man came upon a woman sitting precariously atop the guardrails of a high bridge.

"Don't come any closer," she said over her shoulder to him, her voice tight. "I'll jump."

The man paused for a moment, glancing around. There was no one else in sight. Turning up the collar of his overcoat against the cold, he took another step tentatively toward her.

"I said I'll jump! I mean it."

He studied her face in the moonlight. She was young, nineteen or twenty; her dark hair was swept this way and that by the breeze. Tears glistened on her cheeks. Her eyes were hard with hurt.

She was shivering, underdressed for the weather, as if she had rushed out from somewhere in such an emotional state that she had forgotten completely that it was the middle of winter. Only a pullover sweater, blue jeans, and white open-toed sandals stood between her and the icy December night. The sandals dangled at the ends of her toes as her feet dangled over the guardrails, nothing beneath them but the abyss.

He took another step toward her. She slid herself a few feet away.

"I—I mean it," she insisted, her voice less certain this time.

Their eyes met. She looked away quickly. After a moment he could hear her crying. She was pretty, he thought. Pretty but in so much pain. Unspeakable, intolerable pain.

"He—he said," she wept, "he said that he...And it's—it's Christmas! How could he do—do that—to me—on Christmas?"

She stared out into the depthless night, seeming for a moment to forget the man's presence completely. He took the opportunity to step closer, almost close enough to touch her.

She turned to face him again. "How...?" she whispered. "How—how could he...?"

The man looked at her and shook his head, saying softly, "This isn't the answer."

"Then what is?"

"I don't know. But not this. Come on. You know it isn't."

At last he reached his hand to her. She stared at the hand and her mouth opened slightly, as if in amazement that at this moment of all

64

moments a stranger might appear out of the night to offer her kindness, grace. Their eyes met again. Her face softened.

Finally she reached her hand to his.

When their palms touched—hers was slick with cold sweat—the man suddenly pushed. With a short, surprised scream she slipped from the guardrail and plummeted into the river below.

He stood gazing down at the dark water for some time, his hands burrowed deep into the pockets of his overcoat.

After a while the man walked home with a satisfied spring in his step, humming "Joy to the World" quietly to himself.

After all, he had always wanted to murder a woman.

22. THE MILE LOW CLUB
Rebecca Fung

What's the fascination with joining the Mile High Club?

I suppose there's one real allure – and that's to be able to say you've done it there. You've done it while flying among the clouds.

For some people, just doing it at all is a thrill. I remember my first time, and the frisson that went through my entire body as I realized *I am no longer a child*. But now I've done it in so many places – well, I wouldn't say that the excitement has worn off. I always love it. But the act itself is not enough. I'm looking for something more.

That's when I think of the Mile High Club. I'll do it. It must feel different.

I've never killed someone in the air before.

I'm sitting in the front of the small plane when the idea occurs to me. Strange, that I've flown so many times before – sometimes to a place or from a place where I've completed a hit – but I've never before thought about killing someone in the air. Till now.

The more I think about it, the more irresistible the premise becomes. The spontaneity of the idea attracts and overwhelms me. I'll be in the clouds, and a stranger's life will be in my hands. I love the sensation when you kill someone, you can actually feel their spirit escaping from their body. What perfect symbolism of being airborne while the soul escapes from the victim's body.

I start to plan it. What will be my method this time? I am unarmed. Shooting is efficient and practical in many cases, but it's not my preferred method anyhow. It's a little too clinical and too detached from the actual task.

I like a knife. I like sinking the blade into the back, or slitting the throat. But again – where would I get a knife? I need to be able to improvise. Perhaps I could rustle up something poisonous. I know enough about homemade poisons to do it well, and I do love that look a person has when they realize that death is coursing through their veins. That look of desperation!

But the easiest, I decide, will be strangulation. I have good, strong hands, and all I need to do is walk up to my victim. I wanted to feel the life pass from his body into my hands, and revel in it. A sort of trance then seems to take hold of me, and my rational thoughts disengage.

As if it were some sort of epiphany, I decide, *I'll take the pilot.* How much more power could a murderer feel than when strangling the heart and soul of an airplane while in mid-flight?

I don't think any further on the matter. I could already feel the tingling sensation I get when I'm ready to kill. I walk to the cockpit, find it unlocked, and enter. It's all too easy as I find the interior bolt and lock the cockpit door from the inside, and all the while the pilot speaks to me without turning, assuming that I'm the attendant.

I like to keep things neat and simple, so I step behind him and wrap his neck with the crux of my elbow. He struggles, and I watch. His face changes color and his body cycles through kicking and writhing into limpness. I feel it on his neck, the squirming and jerking of a struggling man, and then the body and the soul give up and his mass falls heavily against my arms.

It is brilliant. My hands are growing larger, drawing energy from his death. I'm grinning. This is power; this is love. My soul soars, and I feel invincible!

Then I return to reality. The plane is dipping. I take the pilot by the collar and thrust him aside, and try to work the confusing panel of the cockpit myself, but I can't make heads or tails of it. The dead pilot seems to look up, his face contorting in a lopsided grin; a smirk perhaps from the other side. *Shouldn't have made such a rash decision, you idiot,* he seems to be saying. *What's your Mile High Club Membership going to do for you now?*

I can hear people screaming and pounding upon the door now. This is the time, I think, when the pilot would come on with a reassuring message, even if it's utter lies, even if he's about to crash them to their deaths, speaking about remaining calm and everything will be ok.

The plane rocks violently and I feel a new thrill as I realize that I'm about to claim dozens of additional lives. *I'm about to crash them and mangle their bodies beyond recognition,* I think with pure joy. If only I could broadcast one of those reassuring fake messages just for sport!

I can hear everyone yelling and screaming and the distraction detracts from my enjoyment. *I can't enjoy your impending deaths amidst all this noise!*

But truthfully deep down part of me has returned to rational thought and I do not truly wish to die this way. Not in a tiny cramped cockpit with the frantic shrieking of others filling my ears. The plane rocks again and I hear a crash, and the blue of the ocean devours us. I hear parts of the hull cave in and rip apart and I feel the cockpit sinking down, down, down…

***

Water. Water is seeping in through the door of the cockpit. It's quiet now. The screams that were unbearable just moments ago are replaced by an eerie silence.

The dead pilot is still staring up at me, his body jammed under the seat and his death gaze peering at me. So odd that the cockpit window didn't break…

My leg is aching dully, and I realize it must be broken. But that doesn't hold my attention now. I'm watching the door to the cockpit. I'm watching the water. I'm watching as the cockpit continues to fill.

Soon it will be full. I lift my mouth above the water now, gasping for what's left of air space to breathe, knowing it will all be gone soon.

And then perhaps I am hallucinating as I'm dying, but I see that a tiny fish is somehow swimming about in the water near me. It swims around the dead pilot, and then past me, unbothered by the wreckage or the rapidly filling death-pit. Uninterested, it swims for the door again. Brazen bastard, mocking me.

I reach out then and grab the fish with my murderer's hands. I can feel it squirming within my fingers and then crush its bones in my grasp.

Ah.

If I'm about to die, I might as well join the Mile Low Club before I depart. Just to know that I've done it.

23. PARTY FAVORS
Chris Leek

Ever since the accident Merv had holed up at the Capri Motor Lodge. Some wise-ass had inked over *Capri* with the word *Crappy* on the sign out front. They had a point. Merv's 'deluxe' room included a cracked sink, a TV with three channels of raging static and a king size bed that shook like an earthquake for fifty cents and dipped in the middle as though a horse had slept in it. Perhaps one did, it was that kind of place. But, once you got used to the rhythm of the neighborhood— breaking glass, sirens and the occasional gun shot—it really wasn't so bad.

Today was Merv's birthday and by way of a celebration he'd scored some dubious looking pills from one of the cracker-heads that hung around the 7-Eleven across the street. The kid had told him they were uppers, but Merv didn't give a shit which way they went.

He'd spent the evening lying naked on the bed, sweating on to the tired mattress and chasing pills with Kentucky's finest. He didn't want company and he certainly wasn't expecting any, but now it seemed like he was going to have some regardless.

They began to arrive in ones and twos. Merv didn't need to count to know there would be 29 in all; one for every year of his miserable existence. That could have just been a coincidence, but even with his brain skimming along on PCP and bourbon he knew it wasn't.

They made a strange congregation, not the kind of people you'd expect to see together. Well maybe in an airport lounge or a bus depot, but not at a birthday party. If that's what this was. The white haired clerk from a Henderson hardware store, a Tasty Freeze waitress out of a Spokane truck stop and a used car salesman from the Valley; you'd struggle to think what they could have in common, but Merv knew well enough. One way or another he'd killed them all.

The first to show up was a kid, not more than ten or eleven. Merv guessed it was Charlie Nichols. His face was all purple and bloated, like it must have been when they fished him out of the Humboldt River in '86. He didn't know Charlie couldn't swim. Hell everyone can swim right? Besides, if his classmate hadn't been such a dick, he would never have pushed him in.

Alongside Charlie stood two Arabs, one with a string of ragged holes across his chest, the other, a single tap to the forehead. Merv was a little surprised to see them here. He was on the Government payroll out in Iraq, although when he thought about it Uncle Sam didn't order him to knock over that little convenience store in Baghdad.

In the corner, was a young Mexican guy, fiddling with the TV antenna. The angry slash across his neck gaped open like a huge toothless grin. Merv didn't know his name, hadn't thought to ask it when he'd car jacked him out on I-80, slit his throat and dumped his body in a dry wash.

Merv shook out a bent Marlboro from the pack on the night stand and leaned forward to accept a light from a Vegas cop. The yellow eyeball resting on Officer Benson's cheek, swung lazily as he struck the match. That heist at Mutual Savings and Loan had gone bad real quick. Merv had talked his way out of murder one and landed an easy five stretch; giving up his partner and convincing the judge that it was Jimmy and not him who pulled the trigger. Sure enough Jimmy was here too, leaning against the wall in his orange prison jumpsuit, the sharpened toothbrush that shanked him still protruding from his neck. It was just like old times, sort of.

Merv reached for the bottle of bourbon, his hands shaking so bad it needed both of them to get it to his mouth. He closed his eyes and sucked down the booze feeling it burning a path down to his guts. When he opened them again Maria and the baby were next to him upon the bed. Unlike the other members of this little gathering Maria still looked like her picture, the one he carried in his wallet. He was grateful there was no sign of the bloody corpse that needed a plasma cutter to free it from the wreck of his Nova. He gazed at the baby girl gurgling contentedly in her mother's arms; a State Trooper had found his daughter twenty yards down the highway in a clump of creosote bushes. Merv screwed up his eyes, trying to block it out, but the show had already started playing again in his head.

He was driving—too fast and too drunk—arguing with Maria over some shit that didn't matter much back then and mattered a whole lot less now. He lost it on a bend, hit the brakes and flipped the Chevy. He walked away without a scratch, didn't even get slapped with a DUI. During all the confusion and carnage nobody had thought to breath-test him. The Devil really did look after his own, only Merv's soul didn't seem worth the price of a family pass.

When he looked up again Maria was gone, in her place were two body bags, one no bigger than a rucksack. Merv realized he was crying. He fumbled around under the pillow and pulled out a rusty .44. The gun

70

had done for a gang banger in a Reno back alley, the same one who now sat in the busted easy chair by the window. Merv bit down hard on the barrel, blinking away the tears. It was getting late, but if he hurried he could still make this party.

24. CAULIFLOWER
Chris Reed

Tony pushed the lunch cart into Mrs. Beechy's room, trying like hell to keep the dishes from shaking. But one of the wheels would barely turn, and he had to lift the back end of the cart off the floor to get it through the doorway. When he lowered the cart back to the floor, the dishes rattled loudly and Mrs. Beechy's eyes popped open.

"Good afternoon, Mrs. Beechy," Tony said, trying to sound cheerful. Trying to sound like he was happy to see the old bitch. But it wasn't easy. She was recovering from hip surgery and she'd been a thorn in Tony's side since the moment she arrived. She complained about everything; her pillow was too flat, the room was too cold, the television too loud. But worst of all was the cauliflower, which she demanded, even though he'd told her the kitchen didn't have any. Mrs. Beechy was, beyond a doubt, the worst patient Tony had ever had to deal with. He constantly had to remind himself not to call her Mrs. *Bitchy*.

"Lunch time," Tony said as he maneuvered the cart to the side of her bed.

Mrs. Beechy sat up, the sagging flesh on her arms wiggling with the effort, varicose veins thick as tree limbs snaking down her legs. Her head was bald except for a few patches of wispy, gray hair, and the wrinkles in her face were deep enough to hold water. According to her chart, she was only eighty-five, but she looked closer to one hundred.

"What kind of crap are you feeding me today?" she grumbled.

Tony lifted the silver lid off the tray and said, "Roast beef and mashed potatoes with a side of carrots."

Mrs. Beechy leaned forward, squinting her ancient eyes. "No cauliflower?"

"I can only serve what the kitchen prepares," Tony said, trying hard not to lose his cool.

Mrs. Beechy slumped back against her pillow with a disapproving scowl on her face. "You got me cauliflower yesterday."

"And I told you it was the last time I could do it," Tony said firmly.

Mrs. Beechy crossed her arms in front of her chest and said, "I won't eat until you get me some cauliflower."

Her defiance infuriated Tony, but he kept his anger in check. "Mrs. Beechy, there's no more cauliflower. What I got for you yesterday was the last of it. Now I can bring you some green beans or—"

"I don't believe you!"

Tony sighed. He knew that if Mrs. Beechy didn't eat she wouldn't get better, and if she didn't get better she wouldn't be discharged. Not only that, but she had threatened to get him fired if he didn't get her the Goddamn cauliflower. She warned him that if he didn't keep her favorite vegetable coming she would tell one of the nurses that Tony had tried to fondle her. She was as crazy as she was old.

So he'd found a way to get her what she demanded. But he didn't know if he could force himself to do it again. The thought of what he'd have to go through made him sick. It made him want to walk right out of the hospital, to quit right then and there. But he needed his job, and the old bag knew it. She knew he'd get her some cauliflower. No matter what.

"I mean it," Mrs. Beechy said. "I won't eat unless I get it."

Tony hated her for her manipulation. He hated her and wished it was her neck that had been broken instead of her hip.

Reluctantly, he grabbed an empty plate from the bottom of the cart and said, "Fine. I'll be right back."

He slipped out of the room, snuck into the bathroom across the hall, and locked the door behind him. If someone walked in and caught him getting the cauliflower, he'd be fired for sure. He reached into the pocket of his scrubs and took out a scalpel and a syringe of Lidocaine - an anesthetic that he'd stolen from the supply cabinet.

Then he dropped his pants and pushed his underwear down to his ankles.

Clusters of venereal warts covered his crotch like stalks of pink cauliflower. The growths were so large that he couldn't even see his penis. A wad of gauze was stuck to his crotch where he had removed a section of the tissue the day before and given it to Mrs. Beechy. She'd devoured it quickly, even commenting on its wonderful taste. Luckily for Tony, she was blind as a bat.

Tony took a deep breath and jabbed the needle into his pelvis. He winced at the pain, an intense heat that spread through his crotch like wildfire. He pushed the plunger down with his thumb, sending the Lidocaine into his groin. Within minutes the pain subsided and his crotch went numb.

He chose a large cluster of warts that was attached to his right testicle and put the blade of the scalpel against its stem. The razor-sharp blade sliced through the tissue with ease. He placed the knot of bloody warts on the edge of the sink, then chose another cluster to sever. This one was attached to the bottom of his testicles and hung there like a second scrotum. He gritted his teeth and slid the blade through the lumpy flesh, separating it from his body.

After patching his wounds with gauze, he rinsed the blood off the pieces of flesh, and then put them on the plate. He pulled up his pants, and returned to Mrs. Beechy's room.

The old woman was still sitting with her arms crossed in front of her. When she saw Tony walk in, she sat up straight, and craned her wrinkled neck out.

"You bring my cauliflower?" she asked.

"Got it right here," Tony said.

He placed the plate on the tray as Mrs. Beechy picked up a fork. She stabbed the largest knot of warts and brought it up to her grinning lips. Tony watched in disgust as the woman chewed his flesh, her false teeth grinding the warts to pink mush.

She swallowed, then said, "You know, you kids these days should be more careful about who you sleep with."

"Excuse me?" Tony said.

"These venereal warts," Mrs. Beechy said, pointing the bloody fork at the last remaining growth on the plate. "They're not the only thing you have to worry about. What about AIDS? And syphilis? You can't get rid of those with a scalpel, young man."

"You knew?" Tony choked, as Mrs. Beechy popped the last bite into her mouth.

"I may be old, but I'm not blind," she said. "And I'm not full, either."

She reached under her pillow and took out a hypodermic needle.

"What's that?" Tony said nervously.

"You're not the only one who knows where the storage cabinet is."

She pushed the lunch cart to the side and got out of bed.

Before Tony could react, the old woman lunged at him, plunging the needle into his neck. He stumbled backward and crashed against the wall, eyes wide with terror, unable to believe what was happening. He reached up and yanked the needle out, but it was too late; the room was spinning and his legs were going numb. Unable to keep his balance, he slumped to the floor as Mrs. Beechy stood over him with a knife in one hand and a fork in the other, her saggy jowls jiggling as she smacked her blood-stained lips.

"I want more cauliflower," she said. "And I know where to find it."

She unbuttoned his pants, and Tony could only pray he'd pass out before she got them off.

25. SICKNESS UNTO DEATH
A.J. French

The palm trees blew outside the window, thrashing in the air, fronds waving. There was a storm coming. A big one. The sky in the west was dark with angry clouds. I took a deep breath, sinking a little further into the chair. I sipped my glass of whiskey. I smoked my cigarette. The dim lamp on the table beside me offered its feeble glow.

Suddenly I laughed. It was all so crazy.

Had it only been three days? It had, but it seemed longer. I felt like a completely different girl. And by the time the storm arrived, I would be gone from this world. That too seemed unreal, fabricated—this idea of leaving. And yet I could not deny it. The creature would soon be there, groping its way out of the palms and deserted foothills that surrounded my home, its last and final pilgrimage to my estate, to enter me, this time with the sole intention of laying waste to my physical body. I shivered, the ice cubes clinking in my glass, and stared into the gathering dark.

Any moment the storm would break.

Perhaps the saddest part of all this was my willingness. Pathetic? Maybe, but I believed it to be more complicated. But that's a euphemism—*complicated*—which we humans use to excuse our own actions. But I was beyond any sense of moral dignity. And I could admit it to myself if I really tried. There was a part of me that *wanted* to be consumed by the beast, in fact *longed* for it, *lusted* for it—like a lover. Sad, yes, but I had had enough of the black and bleak world, and I was ready for escape. The haunting hours of dead loneliness starting immediately in my childhood had pressed steadily down upon me, crushing my spine into submission, until with a bitter grimace I had accepted my reality as an awful truth, with its laws and limits and stipulations. With its soul-crushing *aloneness*. The only gateway I perceived was the gate of death—mine being at the savage end of a bloodthirsty phallus. It was a dance and a seduction. The beast had called—its mating call—and I had answered, and now it would come as it had for the last three nights, only this time it would not come again. And nor would I, for my final extraction from this hollow reality was soon to be completed. The creature would come, displaying its altar of death—its tongue the red carpet, its teeth the pews, its throat the causeway to Hell—and I would bend forth willingly into its divine depths… Ah, to be swallowed so wholly and irretrievably… Yes, it was a seduction, a thing of lovers, a romance, and I would give in.

I would let it come inside me.

I sat very calmly, the house a tomb of silence, pressuring me from all angles. I smoked and I drank (this would require considerable drink, actually). I heard only the wind against the walls and the windows, plus the rustling of the tree branches, and I thought about how vacant and alone I was, how my reality was more dream than vision, a blank jaded nightmare where nothing had ever happened, a landscape of my own malingering imagination, a place for me to bury my hopes in, a charnel expanse of sinking sand and drowning corpses… and so I drank from my cup again, then abruptly I laughed…

…for the storm had broken.

The sky grew purple with twilight and clouds, and the firmament seemed to split like a swatch of fabric, and then the water came down in heavy gray sheets. The lightning stabbed its way eastward, leaving a trail of thunder in its greenish wake, and I smoked my cigarette down to the butt and drank my liquor, watching the rain patterns form on the window.

I heard its mournful call, as I knew I would, a low drawling moan that seeped up from the earth, dispersing into the stormy atmosphere and crashing into the house, rattling it. I stamped out my butt in the ashtray, gulped down my drink, jettisoned the glass, and stood, approaching the window. Spread my fingers against the glass, peering into the hazy gloom, watching, waiting. It came again, the teeth-vibrating moan, and I closed my eyes in private ecstasy.

Finally… my time has come.

With an air of excitement, I exited the back door into the yard, disrobing as I went, down to my bra and panties. The weather had been abnormally hot, and so the drenching rain was still warm as it spattered against my bare skin. But it was cooling down fast, and I was soaked instantly. I could feel my long black hair sticking to my neck and shoulders.

I removed the last of my clothing. My nipples pricked up as they became exposed to the fresh air. The slapping rain felt good, almost sensual, and I swooned, staggering to the swimming pool, where the metallic waters bubbled and rippled. I laid down on the diving board, facing the sky, with my legs splayed. I closed my eyes and waited.

The mating call came again—closer now. I sensed its heavy tread in the vibrations of the diving board, and I could hear the pool water sloshing behind my head. Soon I could smell its fetid presence, its foul physicality, as it drew closer to me, filling up all space and time with its terrible god-like existence. I kept my eyes closed, not wanting to spoil the illusion, not wanting to dilute the experience in any way. I was being subtracted, yes, but I would be born again to a new reality. One less dire and dead-feeling, one where things made sense and had meaning, one that I could feel to be true, goddamn it, one where this horrible soul-crushing aloneness did not permeate all substance—

It stood over me now, looming above my naked fragile form. I had grown wet in eager anticipation of my undoing. The rain slapped at me like a jealous lover and my skin burned and itched. I could hardly stand it for another second.

Do it—do it now! Carry me, rescue me, take me away. Please, I beg of you… Christ, how I ache…

And then it was happening, the creature's immutable presence collapsing down on top of me, pressing me against the diving board with its undeniable weight. I felt pinned to the earth. I felt grounded.

Yes… this is what I want.

It split me apart and cracked me in half, and I felt my inner being pouring out onto the ground, spilling my life essence into an unappealing puddle of sensual wetness and burning hot desire. I could no longer breathe. I felt full of something, something… though I did not know what.

I gave myself over entirely.

"Please…" I whispered up at the storm. "Tear me to bits… so that I may be made whole again. Spare nothing on me… for I chose this punishing escape."

Somewhere in the space above, the creature laughed. And its voice, like a flame of fire, spoke unto me, *"So shall it be… So… shall it be."*

26. BLACK GOLD
Jeff McFarland

Black.

That was the way it always came. As the man stared down into the mug, he became aware of the striking resemblance between the drink and the blackness of oil. Swirling, steaming oil that tainted the pearly white cup with black. A black that was darker than his suit, his tie, and even the spit-polished leather shoes upon his feet.

"Anything else?" the waitress said with more than a bit of disinterest.

The taste was dreadfully bitter, even by this man's standards. But he was not at the moment, able to be bothered with the burden of cream and sugar. Even the appearance of the drink never made him eager for a taste. He glanced at the waitress with a glassy eyed stare that sent pins and needles up her spine.

"No," he replied dryly.

The woman hurried away, mumbling under her breath about 'the freaks in this city.' The man made note of her, and then turned back down to the coffee.

He had been to this establishment several times before, each time because his function had required it of him. Despite his distaste for it, he always followed the routine of the coffee. It was his black gold, and it possessed for him great value.

 The man in black remembered his purpose and turned his attention through the window, toward a bus stop across the street.

There sat two people who caught his attention as they waited upon the bench. One was a middle aged man with a graying beard, and the other a little girl who couldn't have been older than five or six. She giggled playfully, displaying dimples upon her cheeks, while brushing the sandy-blonde hair out her eyes. The man appeared to be telling her a fantastic story, perhaps of princesses or dragons or mermaids.

This sight puzzled the man in black. These people had no fear of their surroundings, despite the run down state of affairs and the apparent gang influenced graffiti behind them. Aside from one another, these two didn't appear to have a care in the world.

As he stared down into his coffee, he realized regrettably that one of them was surely the reason for which he had come here today. He had a quota to meet, and, unfortunate as it was, he was not granted the right to be choosey.

As he mulled these thoughts about in his head, the girl, still giggling at her father's antics, glanced through the window and briefly made eye contact with the brooding man. And then, she did something which no other person had done in the entirety of his substantial work history; she smiled genuinely toward him, and held it joyfully when their eyes met.

The father, taking notice, smiled as well, but then quickly directed the girl's attention away from the window. For the first time in a long while, the man felt the joy of surprise. The waitress who had shuddered at his gaze, the father who shifted uncomfortably in his seat, that was all business as usual. But the girl's sheer fearlessness and enthusiasm for life were things which he had hardly experienced in his line of work. He was still unsure which of them he would be taking, but he had decided that regardless of the outcome, he would do his best to make it quick.

As if on cue, a tremendous gust of wind swooped down and lifted the father's hat from his head, and set it gently in the middle of the street. The man inside tightened his grip upon the cup with hesitant anticipation. The girl's father laughed, got up, and started to make his way into the road. Her father would be an irreparable loss to her, but at least he would feel no pain.

In the black of his coffee, the man saw just how it would transpire. A wife, racked by grief, would never be whole again. A daughter would pass the rest of her life without an assuring word or a warm embrace from the man she called 'daddy.' Her sorrow would grow into resentment, the resentment into bitterness, and bitterness would lead to tragedy. Then it would be the girl that the man came to collect, after a lifetime of poor decisions.

As he reflected upon this, the precocious girl surprised the man in black yet a second time. She raced past her daddy's legs and out into the road to grab his hat. She didn't hear her father yelling out and pleadingly for her to stop. She didn't hear the roar of the engine or the screeching of the tires as the car tore around the corner.

The picture in the darkness appeared differently now: a couple ripped apart by the loss of their only child, a father drowned in alcohol, and a mother left catatonic with depression.

The man in black had seen all that he needed to. He did have an objective to fulfill, yes, but he had never really been one for cruelty. That was best left to his superiors. In the commotion, the noise, and all of the chaos, he uttered one simple word.

"No."

The car screeched to a dead stop, and for only a moment, everything was still. Shocked diner patrons peered out of the windows at the scene. The silence was broken by the father's sobs as he ran and scooped his daughter up into his arms. As he did so, she placed the hat back upon his head and squeezed him tightly. A few of the customers in the diner let out gasps of relief. Others rushed out of the front door to assess the potential damage. And the man found himself glancing down into his coffee mug once again.

Still black. But the images had faded.

The man cleared his throat and peered over toward the counter. "Excuse me," he said. "Could I get some cream and sugar for this?"

The waitress dropped them upon the table and turned without a word. As the man in black stirred them into his coffee, images of her began to appear, and he was reminded of the quota which must be filled.

27. CRUEL MADAME
Naching T. Kassa

Though it was the time of terror, Pierre had only one mistress. Women came to him, offering the delight of their bodies in exchange for life, but he always turned them away. His heart belonged to his Love alone, and he was chaste for her.

She came to him at night, her tread light upon the stairs, the aroma of blood and smoke upon her person. She would climb into his bed, her teeth flashing like a silver blade in the darkness. He would welcome her into his embrace.

They never made love. Their bond was far too ethereal for that. Instead, they spoke to one another. He would tell her of his cause, of the enemies he had accrued, of the people he had saved and she would listen attentively. Then, she would speak of the justice she had done and the mercy she had dispensed. He was rapt in his attention.

Their rendezvous would end just before daybreak, for she had to return home and he needed to continue his work. He would bid a reluctant adieu to his dear one. (The one he always called, "Madame".) And she would leave him with equal hesitance.

During those weeks of endless toil, he lived for the night. He lived for her mahogany tresses and her soft, brown eyes. She was a respite from those who criticized him, who failed to see his vision. When his dearest friend began to question his motives, it was she who lent him the sympathetic ear and supported his reasoning. She always supported him, and it only made him love her more.

And then everything changed.

One night, she came to him and instead of welcoming his embrace, she grew cool within it. When he spoke, she was preoccupied and did not seem to be listening. This continued for several nights.

Then, it happened. She actually questioned him and his views on liberty. He was so offended by her query; he turned away from her and refused to speak. They lay together like two strangers for the rest of the evening.

The next night she did not come.

He lay alone in his bed, waiting for her soft step. At three in the morning, when she had still failed to appear, fear stung his heart. A voice whispered within his mind, speaking a terrifying notion. The truth of it brought him out of bed in a cold sweat. She had found another.

Her strange behavior and her question pointed him in the direction of her new companion. He knew exactly where to go, as he rushed out into the street.

Pierre was right, of course. When he arrived at the home of Anton, his dearest friend, he heard her voice within the walls. A murderous rage filled him and a dreadful revenge began to take shape in his mind. He stole away like a thief to prepare a death warrant.

The next day, he had the roar of the crowd behind him as the wagon entered the square. Anton stood in that wooden transport of death, his hands bound behind his back. Pierre smiled with grim satisfaction. He wondered how his mistress felt now, knowing that the justice she would mete out today would spill the blood of her beloved.

The Judas's death was swift and merciful. When his head was lifted to the crowd, Pierre looked into its surprised eyes with a certain amount of glee. The blood dripped from the clean cut in gentle rivulets. Pierre savored the sight, striving to remember every moment of it.

He was sure she would come that night, but she did not. For hours he waited. At last, he went to search for her.

She was kneeling in the square, when he found her, clad in a scarlet cloak. When he arrived at her side, he saw that she was holding the hand of Anton's headless corpse.

"This was not justice." She said softly.

"I beg to differ, Madame." Pierre replied gently. "He betrayed me. If he could betray his bosom companion, might he also betray the people? Might he also betray all of France?"

"This was naught but envy." She said, as though she had not heard. "You do not wish for justice, you serve only your own peevishness. Anton knew this. He feared for you and the path you had taken. He was not my lover. He simply wished to save your soul."

Pierre could not believe, would not believe her. His heart was wounded because she doubted him.

When she saw that there was no dissuading him, she shook her head with great sadness.

"Oh, Pierre." She whispered. "There is no other way."

He looked up and realized that he was surrounded. The men were his friends or, at one time had been. They closed in upon him.

"Madame!" Pierre cried in terror.

"You forced me to taste his blood." She said sadly. "For the sake of justice, I must taste yours."

The crowd cheered as he was led up the steps to face her, later that afternoon. They called for his death and he frowned at them. They had always hated him.

He looked toward the one who had been his greatest love. Her blade flashed in the sun. She smelled of blood and smoke. He sighed. Even *she* hated him.

But something was amiss with the apparatus that day. It didn't slice cleanly through with the first strike and only pierced into the bones of his neck as he screamed in agony. The second strike silenced his cries, but all of his arteries were not severed and his head lived on weakly for an unprecedented thirteen minutes. The expression on his face was one of pure indignation.

Contrary to Pierre's belief, there was no malice in her action. She was, after all, only an instrument of justice.

Madame Guillotine.

28. TATZELWURM
Nicholas Paschall

Nobody likes me, everybody hates me, guess I'll go feed worms... I hum to myself as I slip beneath the old man's door, the half inch crack more than enough for me to filter through. I can hear the rustling of movement in the darkness, but I'm not afraid.

Just patient.

James Hosenberg, age seventy three as of this last weekend. Lives on the second floor just off of Broadway in Lower Manhattan, acting as the Superintendent for the whole building. I can hear the distant cries of a newborn through the thin walls, as well as a siren in the distance. As I drift across the room, I hear the muttered cursing in Hebrew, and chuckle to myself. The best insults always come from the cultures that have faced oppression, and none have seen it in the same way as Abraham's Children.

Another person rustles deeper in the apartment, his attempts at stealth almost laughable to me. But that's not really fair, as you can't really hide from me for long.

That's because I'm patient.

I can feel the saliva building in my mouth as I can sense the impending meal about to appear, my long tongue whipping past my rows of black serrated teeth. I lower my head to allow one of my short arms to scratch behind my beautiful ears, the other one rotating as I track the noises within the home.

The ticking of an old clock.

The steady, low whistle of the heater.

The rhythmic beating of two hearts, one just before me while the other is slowly approaching.

I float higher, coiling my long tail beneath me, granting me an excellent position to pounce once my meal is available, allowing me to use all six claws and my mouth to bring it down before it can get away.

I can't afford to let it get away. Not this time.

Used to be I got to eat almost three or four times a day, my keen nose picking up the scent of the impending meals before they even realized what their fate was to become.

Now I'm lucky if I get one meal a week, with how fast they move onward.

My eyes gleam in the dark as a sudden bang and a flash of light erupt from the muzzle of a loaded shotgun, blasting a hole through the stomach of a much younger man. I whip my tongue out to catch his scent.

Ahhh… Ernie Hosenberg, age sixteen. James's grandson who was apparently trying to rob the old man of his prescription pain pills, or was possibly just trying to find a place to sleep for the night. I don't care either way.

I watch as the light flicks on and James sees who he's just shot, his wrinkled features going pale at his grandson's prone form and the bubbling pool of blood seeping past his two handed attempt to hold his stomach together. The boy is crying.

I slowly drift over him, waiting for my chance to claim my much-needed prize.

There! The spark of life leaves his eyes as his heartbeat slows to a stop. His grandfather wails, holding his grandson's body as if he could do something to save it. I watch with glee as his soul begins to rise from the boys opened mouth and eyes, drifting and coalescing as I drift beside the weeping elder until young Ernie is now staring at the scene in shock, his ghostly form carrying the fatal wound with it into the afterlife, where he would be treated and judged by his God for his life before moving onto a better (or worse) place.

That is, he would if I wasn't here. I let loose a low growl as I spring onto him, knocking him into the air with a yelp as I sink my oversized mouth over his shoulder, biting into his smoky form and ripping away his vital essence with glee. He punches at me in a vain attempt to dislodge me, but my lower half coils around his legs as my claws begin to rip long wounds across his frame, the wounds bleeding out the cloudy haze that is his corrupted soul. I finish him quickly by engulfing his head and tearing it free, a great puff of smog erupting from the wound before his soul settles, allowing me to eat it at my own pace, to the tune of a weeping murderer.

I begin to hum to myself when his wailing bores me. *Nobody likes me, everybody hates me, guess I'll feed the worms…*

29. DAISY EYES
April Bullard

"What's the big hurry," I whined, as a garter snake slithered across the muddy path. "We've camped on this scraggly, little island for over twenty years." He stopped and turned toward me, holding out his strong, calloused hand.

"Abby, didn't you promise to love and obey?"

A few more steps and I took his hand, as usual. "That was thirty-three years ago, and I said 'o-blay,' through gritted teeth, with my fingers crossed!"

Jim spun me around and wrapped me in a bear hug. He began covering my wrinkled face with little kisses. He made sure his gray streaked beard brushed over every inch and the brim of his baseball cap tapped against my head. "But you love me, and adore me," he teased, "You said so last night!"

"Okay, okay," I chuckled, "I give. What are we looking for?"

Jim released me with a loud, smacking kiss. A raven screeched away from the nearest tree, dropping a single, ebony feather that spun to the ground as if it was trapped in a slow-motion dream.

"Last week, one of the big cottonwoods with the eagle's nest fell during that terrific thunder storm. We've never gone in that part of the woods before. We didn't want to bug the birds."

"Why today? Why now?"

"Because I think I've found the secret we've been searching for, Abby." His mischievous grin grew with a flirtatious wink. "Come on, I'll show you."

I didn't believe him, but I never could resist that boyish curiosity, or that engaging smile. I nodded and fell in behind him, like a faithful sidekick, on the narrow trail. Every few steps I dipped under a low branch, brushing my sleeve covered arms in stands of nettles, or broke berry vines with my jeans and high top boot covered ankles. Jim's clippers squeaked as he widened the deer trail. Each snip answered by angry chirps closing around us. The woods seemed to grow back as fast as he cut it. About twenty minutes and seven winding switchbacks later, we were there.

The fallen moss covered trunk had crushed a huge, tangled mass of blackberry, dogwood, hemlock, thistles and stinging nettle that had formerly blocked our crossing over. Jim leaped onto the lightning charred end of the thirty inch diameter cottonwood log like a mountain goat. He scurried down the column, arms wading through the lower canopy. A screaming face flashed in the sun dappled end of the trunk. I blinked and it was gone.

"Jiminy Cricket, wait up!" I cried out, suddenly feeling very alone and vulnerable.

"You know how I hate that nick name!" He grumbled, scrambling back to me. I traced the outline of the jagged scorched stump with my outstretched hand, not daring to actually touch it. It looked like a cop's hand commanding us to stop. I could still catch a whiff of ozone and smoke off the burned wood palm. A cold tingle traced the hairline behind both my ears.

"Come on, old woman!" He chuckled, and held out his hand, "Out of your rocker!"

I brushed the gray bangs out of my eyes, took his hand and climbed up after him. He spun around and I managed to smack his bottom before he was out of reach. I followed, keeping just enough distance to avoid the back wash of branches in his wake. A huge, green frog belched angrily. He dove into the air, away from my boot, and disappeared in the undergrowth. I tip toed over the moss, carefully stepping around sprays of fern and cream colored mushroom caps. Ahead of me, Jim jumped off the end of the log, more like an agile teenager than a grandfather, and zig-zagged out of sight. Chickadees chided me from both sides. They hopped around just out of arms reach, and bombarded me with alarming chatter. I paused. Goosebumps rose on my forearms. Standing on the plush emerald bridge under pinned, arching branches, with masses of trumpeting birds, felt like trespassing inside of a mythical audience hall of the gods.

"Oh, my god! Abby, honey, you gotta see this!"

I shook off the dark feeling with a nasty shudder. "Coming!" I called, and quickly waddled down the log. Birds blared, "Please, don't go," or was it, "Told you so," peeling away as I passed. I dropped off the end of the trunk and ambled over the winding trail. There was a sensation, a definite sensation, of change as I crossed over.

Jim waited around the ninth bend. He turned to me and put his forefinger over his lips, "Shhhh!" His deep green eyes sparkled with the unbridled joy of a six year old on Christmas morning. I took his hand and stood by his side.

The path opened to a beautiful clearing. Towering cottonwoods, thickly-based with spiked hawthorns and barbed wire-like blackberries bordered the fifty foot diameter meadow that lie in the middle of marsh and quicksand. The floor of the clearing held a solid mass of glowing, white daisies standing four feet off the ground. A magic floating carpet of purest silver, shimmering in the forest filtered sun, tethered to the earth by writhing, stringy green stems. I couldn't move. A low hum vibrated the ground under our feet. Every single daisy turned to look at us.

"Wow!" Jim giggled. A warning thump hit the pit of my stomach. The flowers began to sway in unison. A soft, sweet aroma wafted around us. All the forest noises were silenced. My mind reeled in pleasure.

Jim let go of my age spotted hand and stepped into the circle. "Please, Sweetie, don't," I stammered, "Don't go in there! Don't touch the flowers." He couldn't hear me. My desperate pleas were lost in the void of white petals. He kept walking, trance-like, into the daisies.

My heart pounded against my ribs, pumping ice through my spine. Every twitching muscle screamed, "Run!" But, I could not, would not, leave this clearing without him.

It took five careful steps to catch up to him, trying not to disturb the penetrating glare of the gold-eyed, white flowered stems. I matched his reverent pace. With each footfall, more daisies surrounded us and barricaded us from our forest path, the only escape.

Jim stopped, dead center in the sea of blooms. He bowed his head and closed his eyes. The ground pulsated. Root-like, electric arcs wrapped around our feet. The cottonwoods turned to stone columns. The bushes became statues guarding the meadow. The sky went dead gray. Nothing moved, except the hypnotically oscillating daisies. A whispery lullaby filled my ears. I felt each individual bloom scan us. We were under final judgment in the revived heart of something malevolent, something ancient, something older than humankind. Jim gently leaned side to side, in time with the floral congregation.

"No, Jim! Please, we have to get out of here!" It hurt, as I pried my tingling feet out of the swarming ground currents. The airy tune transformed into a painful buzzing that chain-sawed through my brain. I lunged in front of Jim and gripped both his limp, trembling hands.

"James Nathaniel Burleson!" No response.

"Answer me!" I commanded. His eyes were still closed. The synchronized swaying of the plants spread the haunting, sickly perfume.

"Jim, look at me!" Gently, I placed my forehead against his, and rolled his head up. "Open your eyes," I begged.

His jaw muscles clenched and my forehead retreated, but I remained face to face. Beads of sweat grew on his furrowed brow. His eyelids fluttered open. The reflection of my face was captured in his terrified eyes. Those marvelous flecks of green paled to white streaks. The black pupils grew molten, glowing gold.

"No, Jim!" I sobbed. His hands went cold and stiff.

The earth vibrated. Our feet were cocooned, locked to the ground. The waving horde of daisies blasted a deafening, intricately harmonized fanfare. He was gone. I choked on the thick, fragrant air, keeping hold of his inanimate hands.

I kissed Jim. A perfect, final kiss that surrendered all the love my soul could ever hold unto those unresponsive lips. A tear rolled down my cheek. The world faded to white, and he was gone forever.

30. PARASITIC
C.L. Hesser

Throughout the long nights and desperate hours of early morning, I dread the return of the dream - I dread the resurfaced visage of the creature from beyond the expanse of time, from below the depths of man's most wicked imaginings. It has haunted me throughout my waking hours and possessed my every thought since that night four years ago.

Since the night of the incident my life has been a series of pitfalls, desperate measures and near-encounters with death - the creature exists within and without, dining on my mental capacity until I am left life-weary - little more than an empty shell.

Shattered, I linger now on the edge of mortal death, and to you, my only friend, I pen my final confession, in hope that my soul will find recompense for the act I am about to perform. I cling to your mercy and forgiveness now, at the end of my human existence, and hope that this confession of my sins will grant me safe passage to the afterlife.

I entrust my ultimate testament and my mortal possessions to your care.

In my final hour I dedicate my failing energy to this manuscript. Now - at the end of my struggle - you will be the sole recipient of a tale I shudder to write.

As you well know, having been in my confidence since the years of our formal education, I have long been of the belief that paranormal phenomena have little basis in reality.

My friend, I wholeheartedly recant my previous philosophy - these years I have spent in isolation, tormented by a being belonging to the dark side of human conception, have stripped me of any notions I formerly held concerning inexplicable phenomena. The monster - even now, as I clutch to my breast the deadly belladonna, desperately composing my final testimony - looms before me, flings its shivering tentacles akimbo.

Its millions of lidless eyes bore into the vestiges of my soul, seeking out and feasting upon my very essence. Its thick, purple tongue wags from between slack lips, black and slick with putrid blood. Undulating, grey flesh writhes before my very eyes, expanding in boil-like pustules to press precariously against the walls and ceiling.

Trusted companion, I am beyond help. The creature before me grows stronger.

I cannot tarry in dedicating to paper an account of the night - in hope that no one else will meet the end which rapidly rises up to consume me, and I pray you will now understand why I must take my own life while it is my own to take.

***

My first night before the onslaught of wakeful misery - the twenty-fourth of June, year 1943 - fell like a funereal shroud of blackness upon the village and surrounding countryside.

Out of the dark, the piercing, inhuman cry of a madman reverberated through the night air - my brother, the lunatic. We'd caught him up in his bedchamber, where he then interchangeably roared like a caged beast or mewed like a broken kitten.

I kept my post at his door - my lonely vigil punctuated by his enraged screams - into the small hours of the night, terror and sorrow intermingling in my mind while he raged within the shadowy bedchamber. As the fourth hour of my night watch peaked, the tremor of his voice abruptly lowered to a wavering quiver, barely perceptible through the bolted door.

I heard him curse softly from within, and then begin to plead vehemently to a mysterious presence, unseen by myself. His voice rose and fell in a soft, furious, desperate flood of indiscernible words, and as I watched anxiously the door, a figure paced upon the floor before it, shadowy footsteps plodding quietly across the woven rug.

As the rapid flow of words died away on his tongue, I crept to the keyhole, and pressed my ear to the metal. I waited a few moments, still as the grave, and as he did not utter a sound or make any palpable movement, fear began to creep into my heart. My hand curled unconsciously about the cool doorknob, and I paused as his voice rung out mournfully in the disheartening silence, calling my name once.

"Yes," I said. "I'm here, brother."

I pleaded entry when he slipped back into silence. After a moment, I slightly opened the door and slid my thin figure through the gap into the small, darkened room. In a sudden movement I shut the door behind me, locking it once again with the key I kept within my shirt pocket.

The window pane stood open, curtains astray. The rain soaked through the books piled up upon the sill - the pages logged with murky water. The candelabra, now extinguished, lay on the Oriental rug in the midst of a burnt hole. I saw the sheets crumpled nearby, which he'd apparently used to smother the fire before it had come to my attention. The bed covers, torn from the mattress, lay strewn about the floor, and his papers had been littered about the chamber, scattered haphazardly from the desk.

My brother's massive form hunched over the bed, ruddy hands clasped together like a child lisping his prayers at his mother's knee; his lips moved noiselessly, shaping words whose portent I could not assume to know. I moved to touch his shuddering figure, and he clenched his fists together, bared his teeth, then he regained a calmness of countenance and motioned for me to crouch down beside him and lend him my ear.

I took my place by his side and he murmured to me an unintelligible muttering. I leaned closer until I could feel his hot breath on my face, my brow furrowing and the corners of my mouth twitching in concentration.

I sensed, then, a separate entity in the room – and as my brother's eyes locked on mine, devoid of reason, and his lips trembled perceptibly, the great tentacle appendages of the beast swung up, thrashing, at his back. In my peripheral vision the creature slashed wickedly to his throat, eyes ablaze with wild animal fury.

***

From here on, I speak speculatively - but I believe that in passing, my brother willed to me the parasitic beast, desperate to rid himself of the monstrous burden. My own life force, now, has dwindled in the past years, and I have isolated myself from others so that I cannot, in dying, pass on this terrible affliction.

The creature will torment me, not relenting until another is near enough to take my place; I have allowed myself to be tortured in order to preserve you, and I hope no-one will be near enough at my death that the beast will cling to them.

My friend, I must leave you now.

I die, remember, an honorable death.

31. THE THING IN THE RIVER
J. T. Seate

It hid in the depths of the river, or in the reeds along the banks, or pretended to be floating waste while it watched…and waited.

In this age of Jesus sightings in a potato chip or the Virgin Mary on a piece of French toast, there was little in Debra's life to surprise her. But, this was different. This wasn't something conjured from an overactive imagination. This was real.

Over the years, she'd seen the monster a dozen times or more, first with her parents and later with a girlfriend or boyfriend. When she was younger, she imagined it to be some kind of half-man and half-fish, the male version of a mermaid. As she grew into a woman, she feared it might be something more sinister, something that could bite. Still, in all the times she'd been in the river, it had never harmed her, so she still came to the same shallow place along the riverbank and swum in the ambling current of the refreshing stream.

With every crisis, Debra had taken refuge at the water's edge. It was her way of escape. She never came alone, however, for she couldn't be absolutely certain about the intentions of thing in the river. The shadowy form she occasionally saw beneath the water's surface told her it was the approximate size of a man, or a gator, but there weren't any alligators or crocodiles in her little corner of the world.

She often took moonlight swims in the buff. Her eyes would flicker with specks of moonlight lifted on a wave of infatuation as she would stand where it was shallow enough to arch her back as if she were offering her torso to the heavens while the stream divided around her, a landlocked mermaid as statuesque as the figurehead on a sailing ship. She sometimes reached toward the sky as if a trapeze might magically appear and carry her away. Sometimes she would see the dark shape in the water, and sometimes she wouldn't, but she knew it was there and wondered if it would eventually make itself known. Her escorts have never been able to see it.

Finally, there came a particularly trying evening in which she headed for the river by herself. It was a sultry night, and she'd had a little too much to drink. She came to the spot at the water's edge which she always frequented. Sitting along its bank, she beckoned to whatever hid in the river to reveal itself. Except for Debra's breathing and the beating of her heart, the only sounds came from the tranquil movement of water and that of the night creatures singing their haunting melodies, looking for a companion, perhaps.

A loon suddenly voiced its lonely cry. Surrounded by a sky as black as a night in hell, the moon shone on the water, looking down with a vapid eye, pouring its light onto things better left hidden. Then Debra heard a new sound.

"Debraaa," it sounded like, barely more than a whisper, carried along on a gentle breeze.

Her eyes scanned the river's darkness, staining to see. There was…something. It had risen from the river's center, the upper torso of something not quite human. Her instincts told her to run, but she was held captive by her curiosity. The thing that swum near her for years had finally decided to display itself. She was spellbound and the need to solve this mystery was stronger than her fear. The dark shape emerged from the water, glistening and raw. It came closer, silhouetted against the silvery expanse of the river, closer and closer, but still too far away to discern its features.

"Debraaa," the thing whispered again.

Debra stood and stepped out of her dress. Her naked body was a map of uncovered treasures. She slipped off the bank into shallow water. Wavelets of foam curled around her ankles like Medusa's snakes. She waded in up to her knees.

"Yes, it's Debra," she said softly. "Who are you? What are you?"

"I'm the thing in the river, what's left of a man who drowned upstream many years ago. They never found me, but I found you. I've wanted you all this time, but you've never come alone…until now."

Debra stood frozen like the ship's mast she sometimes impersonated. An arm reached forward and a hand grasped her shoulder. She could see him now, a mass of wet, hanging strips of decomposed skin, empty sockets where eyes should have been; his mouth, a jelly-like, rancid maw.

"Mine at last," the voice gurgled.

She caught a gamey whiff of the creature and her mouth opened to scream, but all that came out was a stifled croak. This fleeting moment was all she was given before being pulled into the river with the thing. The two dark figures disappeared into the depths of the river, flowing downstream amidst the current, as the loon cried out beneath the impassive moon.

32. TESTAMENT OF FLESH
Bruce L. Priddy

I braved clouds of bot-flies to bring Beth dinner, cotton stuffed in my ears, shirt pulled over my nose to keep the bugs out. They would burrow into any exposed orifice. An animal had died in the library's air-ducts weeks earlier. Maybe. The janitors had yet to find it. Every day the stench worsened and the infestation with it. The university had even been forced to close the school library.

But Beth refused to stop working. She restored rare manuscripts for a living, safely in a climate-controlled room. She had been handed what she called a restorationist's dream, the last extant copy of a Greek book thought lost to the pyre in 1050, upon order of the Patriarch of Constantinople. The university purchased the book at auction after the remnants of a library were discovered in a forgotten cellar. It was the former home of a prominent 18th-century Providence businessman killed by a mob after accusations of witchcraft. Three-centuries of neglect had ravaged the book. The text was fading to a state that was nearly unreadable, and entire sections were missing. Both the spine and the cover were consumed with mold.

Beth did not just work on the book, she obsessed over it. She left her office only when I coaxed her out. Often she passed out where she sat, surrounded by the more recent and error-ridden versions which had been translated into other languages before the Patriarch's suppression of the tome. I'd carry her home and she would whisper in her sleep, reciting couplets from that damned book. When I'd wake she'd already be back at the office. She bathed only once a week or so, and only if I urged her. She only ate when I brought her food. Already thin, she'd become gaunt, all color leeched from her skin. Trying to talk to her about my concerns resulted in the worst fights of our marriage.

I found her standing in the back of her dark office, naked, her whole body covered in what appeared to be bloody scratches. Fearing she'd been attacked, I dropped the food and ran to her. Then, I saw. Those were not scratches, but red ink running beneath her skin. Her eyes rolled, displaying wide circles the color of parchment. She swayed, croaking the noises of a night-insect. I reached out to her. "My God, baby, what did you do to yourself?"

Beth grabbed me, forced my head to her breasts. She screamed one word in a dozen languages all at once. "Read!" Words formed and flowed across her. Arabic, Latin, Greek, English. Couplets, passages, entire chapters. She was a testament of flesh. I shut my eyes against the burning words and threw myself away from her. Clumps of my hair came away in her hands. I am not ashamed to say I ran.

When I returned with the police, Beth was gone. The book lay where she last stood, restored. The cover rough with the outline of the lips I'd known for years, contorted in a scream. Each page was soft as her skin, each bore her freckles, her dimples…

33. LOVER'S LAMENT
Marc Shapiro

Cyril and Angelique were engaged in the act of coitus. She was lean, statuesque, and beautiful, with long flowing blonde hair. He appeared ruggedly European, well-muscled and angular.

"Just like a romance fable come to life," thought Cyril as he nibbled at her neck while thrusting forcefully between her legs. "Even the canopy bed and the flickering candles are perfect."

Cyril looked intently into Angelique's eyes. They were lustful and loving in their intensity. "I love you, thought Cyril." But his eyes had now lost their passion and heat. In their place were sadness and resignation.

"But I want to live," he thought.

Cyril's body was still enraptured by the sexual heat and the vigor in which Angelique returned his lovemaking. But his mind was now filled with the centuries passed, and a thousand lifetimes among them.

"So he consciously put aside those memories, and recalled with clarity the images of the Euro trash nightclub weeks ago, and how he had spotted her across the crowded dance floor. She looked uptown sophisticate and seemed to be searching for...

"This moment," thought Cyril.

Locked together, their eyes explored each other's souls; the sexual tension that lit up the night; from the moment he had taken her hand.

"The look. The caress," remembered Cyril as their bodies continued their dance. "Driving through the night, the wind in our hair, the wanton gleam in her eyes. We were already mentally bound within a lover's trance."

A shuddering orgasm and Angelique's scream brought Cyril back to the present. And then the rush of his own physical pleasure that took him back...

To the memories. The lovemaking on The Rhine. Dancing until dawn on a full moon Paris night. The sealing of so many bonds with a passionate kiss.

Cyril had hoped Angelique would be the one. And for quite a while, she was.

But when you live forever, bonds fatigue quickly. When sex is all that you have you realize that you are truly the living dead...

"And I want to live," sighed Cyril, emitting silent frustration as a tear rolled down his cheek. He moved his head slowly, tenderly, toward Angelique's neck. These weeks past it had been the prelude to a kiss and so much more. But it was time to go their separate ways.

The fangs came out and eased into her jugular. And he cried as he consumed her essence.

Cyril stood over her, eyeing both the pleasure and the agony on his dead lover's face. He began to contort and spasm, his own sense of euphoria that came with the rush of blood sedation. His leathery wings emerged and unfurled. He was drawn, half man, half beast out into the darkness. Sadness marked his monstrous face.

"And now to move on once again," the monster sighed as it climbed to the open window, tasting the breeze as it peered off into the night. Its wings arched to a full span as it prepared for flight.

"Off to another life."

Cyril looked back a final time upon the lifeless, bloody form of Angelique. His tears flowed anew as he leapt silently through the open window.

"And to another love."

34. ROBERT
Charles David Bennett

He lived alone and, for the most part, the only conversations he ever had were with the voices in his head. He lived in a drunken stupor much of the time, and was flat-out inebriated most of the time. He was a loser and he knew it, though, he didn't much care.

With his life facing impending disaster and probable doom, this father of two was utterly alone. He had two daughters from two former failed marriages, though he no longer knew the girls at all. His father was long dead from heart troubles, and his mother and brother both dead of Huntington's Correa. He was the very definition of abandoned and alone; even his sanity had departed. His name was Robert. (I'll strike his last name from the record as this tale is not entirely fictional. Besides, it's my story and I can do what I want with it, pfffft!)

Robert lived in a shit-hole second story apartment in sector twenty-three of one of the larger metropolises in the state. This ghetto was so wretched with villainy that even the police would rarely venture into it. Robert was a slob in the most extreme manor with fetid, rank dishwater in the kitchen sink, old spaghetti stuck to the walls, half eaten hotdogs violating overflowing ashtrays and so on. He would sit in the gloom, amid his own feces, and masturbate. He would scream at the walls or punch holes in them, and from these vibrations, one of the many stacks of empty beer cans would occasionally fall over. These were the only real sounds in his miserable life.

Robert was quickly losing the past pieces of his mind, and this was surely accelerated by the action of his sister putting a gun in her mouth and splattering her brains across her living room wall. I know this to be true, as I, and several other friends, were there to help clean up the remainder of the mess after the police hazmat team decided they had done a "good enough" job.

Robert saw twisted demonic faces in just about everything he looked at. He referred to these things as 'Spooks', 'Demons', and at times 'Evil Bitches'. He'd complain, to the very few people who looked in on him, that these 'Evil Bitches' would play with his privates, and try to rape him during his restless sleep.

I jokingly said to him once, "It's just your left hand dumb-ass!" And because of this quip, he had gotten violent with me, and I had to knock him to the ground.

In reality, however, these voices, spooks, demons, and the like, were nothing more than schizophrenic hallucinations. The latter fed off of Robert's fears, anger, unrequited love and became a violent thing of shadow---A splintered mirage if you will---slithering through the dark waters of his mind.

And it was with the above mentioned circumstances that Robert awoke one day to the screams of a young girl in the neighboring apartment being raped by her drunken stepfather.

"SHUT UP DEMON!" He screamed at the bedroom wall. Ambient light invaded his second story bedroom windows and reflected off the beads of sweat on his bronze skin. His apartment held the usual bouquet of stale spilled beer, piss, cigarette smoke and the sweaty, pungent odor of unwashed human. He groaned as he sat up.

"Bitch", he muttered, as his yellowed eyes slowly roamed to the bottle of 'Heaven Hill Brandy', a knight in shining armor sitting atop his dresser. Standing, spastically jerking and bending at such angles that it would make you wonder how he never threw-out his back, he staggered toward the bottle with arms outstretched as though he were a drowning man reaching frantically for a life line.

He took several long pulls from the bottle, and then in a fit of coughing, slammed the bottle back down on the dresser. Some of the bottles precious brown fluid erupted from the impact, spilling upon the eroding varnish.

He staggered into his living room and slammed his ass down into his tattered easy chair. Still bending side to side and shaking severely he took a smoke out of his mangled cigarette pack and, holding the lighter with both hands, attempted to light it.

"I'LL SLIT YOUR FUCKING TROAT BITCH!" He screamed; the cigarette fell from his lips.

I heard him yelling through his door, and I thought of turning and leaving. I had come over to check on him due to the unusually hot summer, and because everyone else had given up on him completely. The radio was blasting in the neighbor-girl's apartment. Lobotomatic's 'Fist City' had just concluded and the first urgent notes of Gunslinger's 'If The Bombs Don't Get Ya, The Bullets Will' began. (The two songs were hymn's to the poor souls who were forced to live in the massive ghetto). Like I said, I thought of leaving, but knocked anyway.

"BITCH," I heard him say as he flung the door open, flipping me off at the same time. He looked like a demented Santa Claus, with his long white scraggly hair and full beard that contained a cargo of potato chip crumbles.

"Hey, Robert, what's up?" I said as I entered the shit-hole apartment. He mumbled some nonsensical jargon, and then:

"Got a cigarette?"

"Nope," I thoughtlessly replied. You had to always tell him no with the cigarettes, otherwise he'd smoke your whole pack in twenty minutes. As he fell back into his chair, a herd of cockroaches stampeded out from underneath it. I shivered.

"Got twenty quid I can borrow?" He asked. Robert never paid anyone back.

"No. And even if did," I lied, "I still couldn't afford to give it to you for cigarettes and beer," I said, noticing the warm case of 'Bullfrog Beer' next to his chair.

"I need it to help me fight the demons," he replied.

"I've told you a million times, the only demons you have is all the alcohol you consume. You need to see a doctor!" I yelled. The pupils of his dull blue eyes became parasympathetic after I spoke this. I knew he was going to get combative with me and I took the fighting horse stance to await his attack.

He launched his six foot two inch frame at me.

"YOU DON'T BELIEVE IN DEMONS!" He screamed, face as red as a beet and arms flailing.

I used a simple kimono grab on him as we met, and flung him through the open door and down the steep flight of stairs. He landed at the base with an undignified sound. His neck was at an impossible angle and I knew he was dead.

"Ignorant bastard," I muttered to no-one in particular, and felt then my brain somehow changing. It was a scattering of sorts, as my thoughts became fragmented and I could not quite connect them together in a rational order.

I un-shouldered my back pack then, ripped open the case of warm beer upon his floor, and stuffed the pack full of cans. I then fled the building as though a trail of gunpowder were pouring out my ass and an angry torch-lit mob were to the rear. I made my way through the shadows of the darkening streets, past the boarded-up hulk of Harry Harrison High School, and finally made safe port back at my hide.

***

It's the dog days of summer now, the silly season, and the setting sun did little to ease the insufferable heat. My box fans labor hard circulating the humid air, as I sit in my fifth story window drinking the warm beer and smoking stale cigarettes and reveling in their foulness.

From somewhere, in the building across from me, a radio is singing of harbor lights. Two floors down, some asshole is screaming and beating his wife. Oh and the cats, they are fucking and fighting down in the alleyway. A distant dog is barking at some unseen hoodoo, while over the white noise of the fans, I can hear the streets with its gunfire and cars. Sweat falls into my eyes and burns like hell, and I curse the droplets, then wipe them away with my filthy tee shirt.

Sighing I lay down on my bed and watch a cockroach make crystal dung tracks across the wall. In the cacophony of madness I roll over and fuck my atomic alarm clock.

35. URBAN LEGEND
J. T. Seate

It had been a bad day for Grace, and after leaving her office building, it got worse. She glanced over her shoulder looking for a dark shape slipping from behind garage pillars to parked cars. Sometimes her overheated imagination messed with her perceptions. Before climbing into her car, she checked the well of the backseat. Once inside, she locked the doors and pulled away from the day's concerns, or so she hoped. The scariest scene Hollywood ever produced was where some monster slowly sat up behind a driver ready to commit whatever terrible atrocities the script called for.

Another dark night and another drive from town to her cozy cottage. Grace fought the urge to check her rearview mirror in spite of her backseat ritual. She'd made it hundreds of times without incident, but this time things felt eerier than usual. She tried to chalk it up to pressure at work, or the investment into her current relationship. She felt her mind drifting, not quite in control of the sensations she was feeling and the doubts she had.

Wind began to whip the trees along the roadside. The darkness evolved into rain clouds. The drops spattered the windshield and roof of the car like a vicious, stabbing assault from above. Approaching headlights peered from the rain like maniacal phantoms with blazing eyes. Even the swish of the wiper-blades was chilling. *Be-ware, be-ware,* they seemed to hum as Grace pondered how thoroughly a tiring day could screw with your psyche. She saw her eyes reflected in the rearview and the early stages of fright within them. Once fear got started, it had a way of taking hold. The air in the car was suddenly stifling. A sense of suffocating fed her panic.

She needed to think happier thoughts like when the backseat of a car had been friendly, with some lover during college. The memory brought a pleasant respite because she and Tom had been getting along poorly. They hadn't spoken for a couple of days. If and when it came, make-up sex would certainly help to shed the stress demons.

It seemed like an eternity before she reached her street, but the rain had stopped by then. The backseat remained quiet. Thank goodness for little favors. She relaxed at the sight of her porch light powered not by human hands, but by a $12.99 automatic timer purchased at the local Target. Lights flickered within houses up the block, showing signs of life she was grateful to see. A man stood on the street corner wearing an evening jogging suit. A neighbor woman in a nightgown was fetching her dog to stop his yapping at the jogger. Normal enough activities, but her anxiety still lingered. Only one course of action when she felt this way: just wash her face, take a sleeping-pill, and climb into bed, sadly alone.

Grace's headlights swept into her driveway. The garage door rumbled open and she pulled inside. She shut off the ignition and listened; nothing but the sound of the engine clicking as it cooled. With a sigh, she climbed from her car, opened the door leading to the kitchen, and flicked on a light.

Something didn't feel right. A dim shadow stood against the far wall of her living room. *But it must be just another figment of her overindulgent brain.* Gooseflesh rippled up her arms. She had no pets to scurry around the house. The shadow was unquestionably human. She put her hands over her mouth to hold in a scream. The hair on the back of her neck felt like crawling spiders.

Grace turned and bolted back toward her vehicle. Thank God she hadn't yet closed the garage door. The monster that wasn't in the backseat had become the monster in her house. With keys in hand, she pulled open the car door, engaged the engine, and quickly backed down the drive to the street. Barely glancing back at her house, she sped away.

After driving to what she considered a safe distance, she pulled over and tried to quiet the roaring in her head. She fished her cell phone from her purse. The little screen lit the darkness. She punched in 911, reported an intruder inside her house, and gave her address. She must call Tom, tell him what happened, and drive to his place. Everything would sort itself out in his arms.

Her phone suddenly purred. She pushed the talk symbol.

"Hello?"

Tom's voice. "Grace? What the hell? Where the heck did you go?"

"What?"

"Why'd you take off? I was waiting."

"In the dark?"

"I have a key, you know. I wanted to make up by surprising you."

Grace's shoulders relaxed, allowing the weight of fear to fall off. She felt both relieved and embarrassed as a patrol car's headlights on the way to her house made her squint.

"Tom, you better put your clothes on if you're undressed. The cops are on their way."

"Jesus, Grace!"

"I'll be there in a minute. Please don't get yourself shot in the meantime." She closed the phone and imagined Tom sheepishly coming out to face police officers, but then it would be all right, a bizarre ending to a difficult day. Her face found the shadow of a smile. The sweet anticipation of what would follow produced a sigh of relief.

Grace turned the ignition switch. The car creaked slightly. She heard a muffled thumping sound…like a fist against the inside a coffin lid…or…feet moving in the well behind her. She glanced into her rearview mirror. A figure loomed on her backseat, a jogging jacket with the hood pulled up, a specter from her deepest fear, in the flesh.

Her terror searched for answers. Man on corner. Open garage door. In the wrong place at the wrong time. She caught a whiff of the monster's sweat as her mouth opened to scream, but all that exited was a stifled croak. There was no safe haven to prevent her worst nightmare from becoming what urban legends feed upon.

36. THE ITCH
Julianne Snow

It started as an itch.

Just above his appendectomy scar.

A niggle akin to a tickle, then a full-fledged insistence.

Powerless to control the urge, Scott raked his jagged fingernails like scythes over the spot.

The more he scratched, the more persistent the urge became. Like an addict, he continued to collect his epithelial cells beneath his unkempt nails.

The night seemed endless with the constant itch in his side. He continued to dig deeper into his flesh, hoping to scrape out the source. Rubbed raw within the first hour, he realized that it would only take longer to heal. Yet, he continued to serve his annoying master. Too lazy to get out of bed to check his corpulent flesh, he resigned himself to the fate of a potential scar. Even in his restless sleep, his fingers sought out the now tender spot of raw skin.

***

In the morning, Scott awoke feeling groggy and thick-headed after a night spent tossing and turning. Taking his time to get out of bed, he absentmindedly scraped at his side. Feeling a stickiness, he pulled his hand away from his side and tried to focus on the tips of his fingers. Red. Blood? Had he really scratched that hard?

Coming to the realization that he'd done some real damage throughout the night, he made his way into the bathroom to stand before the mirror over the porcelain sink. Looking at his expansive belly in the reflection, he was aghast at what he saw.

Slowly oozing red blood and a viscous, unctuous clear fluid, the patch on his abdomen was larger than he had first imaged. *Had he really scratched a hole in the side of his body?* It was incomprehensible to Scott that he could have done this much damage overnight. Something had to be wrong; there must be an explanation...

After placing a quick call to work, he dressed and left for the hospital, silently praying that whatever he'd done to himself could be undone.

***

Alone in the stark cubicle, replete with a pale blue dotted gown that wouldn't close over his ample ass, Scott sat on the uncomfortable hospital bed, feeling the itching of his side worsen. The admitting nurse had taken one quick look at it and immediately set him up in a room with the inadequate gown. Upon her exit, she added that the doctor would be with him shortly and promptly shut him off from the other patients by closing the pale green curtain.

The fear was all consuming. What the hell was wrong with him? Scenes from the past few days played over and over in his head. He ran through the multitude of people he'd encountered; his co-workers, the pizza guy, the pretty check-out girl at the supermarket, even the woman he visited once a week to satiate his desires. He raked his mind for clues as he raked at his flesh; could one of them have infected him?

The more he thought about it, the more his mind dwelt upon the possibilities.

The more he pondered, the deeper he scratched.

The only thing that broke his reverie was the middle-aged, balding doctor that pulled back the curtain. He strode in with outward purpose and an undercurrent of apathy. Not glancing up from the chart in his hand, he stopped by the edge of the bed.

"What seems to be the problem, Mr. Harris?"

"Well doc, I have this itch on my side –"

"An itch, Mr. Harris? You came to the ER for an itch?" He mumbled something about a prescription ointment and turned to leave the room.

"What?! You're leaving? You haven't even seen –"

"Seen what? Some patch of skin that has you scratching? Let me see it then, go ahead and lift the gown."

He stupidly fumbled with the side of the fabric, trying desperately to pull the corner of it from under his thick thigh. Finally extricating the gown, he lifted the edge to reveal his swollen belly with the rawness of his abdomen.

For a moment, it looked as if the doctor might apologize for his outburst. Instead, he placed the chart on the bed beside Scott and bent forward for a closer look.

Just as quickly, his head jerked back, surprise covering his face. Turning to the small desk, he opened a drawer and pulled out a skinny metal probe about the length of a pen.

"I'm just going to apply a little pressure, Mr. Harris. Nothing to fear, just need to take a better look…" His words trailed off as he advanced the probe at Scott's stomach.

Scott felt a tiny bit of pressure deep inside his stomach and then a fluttering. It was a strange feeling and one he couldn't recall ever having experienced before. Not painful, but uncomfortable.

The doctor's hand retreated almost immediately, searching for something. He found it by the wall next to the desk and promptly vomited into it. Wiping his mouth with the back of his hand, the doctor turned to look at him, fear and revulsion painting a picture of horror across his face.

"What is it Doctor? Am I going to die?" The fear in the room was palpable. Scott sat bewildered and afraid for his life, and the doctor now afraid of his patient.

"You'll have to wait here a moment, I need a second opinion." Almost breaking into a run, the doctor left the cramped cubicle, leaving behind the stench of vomit and burned coffee.

Within moments he had returned, a pretty young blonde haired doctor in tow. She smiled warily at Scott and introduced herself. "Hello, Mr. Harris. I'm Dr. Campbell. Would it be alright if I had a look at your side, please?" She asked with a politeness that almost made up for the way that the other doctor had behaved.

"Sure…" he answered, "Just tell me I'm going be okay and I'll show you anything." The comment was a bit off color, but Scott was a warm blooded male; even in sickness. Bending down, she stared at the spot on his side, intently trying to make out what she was looking at. After a moment her head jerked back suddenly, her hands coming straight up to her face.

"Oh my God."

"What? What is it?"

"See? I told you…"

"But that's impossible. There's no way that-"

"No way that what? Could someone please tell me what's going on?"

Again, Scott felt the stirring within his stomach. Reflexively, he placed his hand on his side and rubbed. Only this time he could feel something new.

Smooth. Hard. Tiny. Square. And now there was a definite hole.

"Mr. Harris, you may want to move your hand-"

The pain was excruciating. His fingers were on fire. He removed them from the wound to have a look, and was shocked to see what he could only interpret as teeth marks marring the surface. Teeth? Was that what he had felt?

Remembering the tiny bathroom he'd passed on his way to the cubicle, Scott moved faster than he'd ever moved before. With the edges of the gown flapping behind him, he threw the light switch and ripped the fabric across his stomach to get a better look. The sight astounded him.

He had a mouth on the side of his abdomen. A fully formed mouth with teeth, lips and tongue. Looking more closely, he could see a faint swell that had begun to form above the mouth, along with twin semi-circular arches of coarse black hairs exuding from the skin above.

Feeling sick, he turned to the doctors who had followed him down the hallway, anguish and confusion now covering his face.

"That's a mouth right? A fucking mouth on my side?"

"Yes, Mr. Harris. We believe that's what it is."

"How the fuck did it get there?"

"We have no idea, Mr. Harris. But that could be the least of your problems-"

"The least of my problems? I have a fucking mouth - with teeth – on my stomach. What the hell could be worse?"

The two doctors shared a glance, "Well, it doesn't appear that it's just a mouth-"

As soon as the words were out of her mouth, Scott's world went dark and he crashed to the ground.

***

Waking up in the hospital was an eerie feeling; part of his brain remembered the horror that had felled him, while the other maintained that it was just a bad dream. Trying to move, Scott realized that he couldn't. Panicking, he fought to adjust and shift, believing that he was now paralyzed with that thing on his stomach. Turning his head to the left, he saw that a restraint covered his wrist. He strained against it, testing it, then realized that it would be hopeless to struggle.

Looking to the right, he saw that his other wrist was also bound. Recognizing the futility of struggling, he laid he head back down on the pillow. Breathing deeply for a moment, he began to take stock of everything. His left leg hurt, as did his left shoulder. His head was pounding but Scott attributed that to the fall he now realized he had taken. His mind then returned to the true horror.

The mouth. With all of its little white pearlescent teeth.

Shuddering, he strained his head upwards, attempting to see the side of his abdomen. Letting his head fall back down in defeat, he started to

110

cry. He had no idea what was happening and it terrorized him. And why were there no doctors here to console him and speak of the cure?

The wait for someone to come was interminable. When a doctor finally arrived, Scott opened his mouth to speak, but no sound came forth. The terror of that moment was profound.

"Mr. Harris, you need to calm down. Getting yourself all worked up isn't going to help you at all."

Again, Scott tried to speak; his mouth opening and closing with each attempt. Frustrated, he began to sob.

"Mr. Harris, it will be all right. We have you scheduled for surgery later today. Once we remove the tumor, everything should go back to normal. These types of things happen all the time. One of the unique things about the cells within our body is that they have the ability to develop into any of the body's structures. It's simply an anomaly, however unfortunate it may be." With a reassuring hand on his arm, the doctor gave a small squeeze before leaving the room.

He desperately wanted to accept the explanation, and tried putting his mind to rest. At least the itch was gone. And soon the growth would be as well. Closing his eyes, he thought about the glorious void of sleep, hoping to drift off into a world that was free of the hell which he currently experienced.

As he nodded off, a small graveled voice spoke aloud and awoke him, "But I'm not a tumor…"

37. GONE AWRY
Adam Millard

I've forgotten my umbrella. I could kick myself; she specifically instructed me to bring one. I have no idea what she looks like, and now the chances of our meeting successfully have severely diminished.

It's not even raining, though. Surely I'd look foolish, standing here on the street corner with an umbrella. Wouldn't it have been easier to exchange photographs or at least descriptions so that we might identify one another? I'm starting to think she must be unattractive, ashamed of her appearance to the point where revealing herself to me beforehand would sway my decision to rendezvous with her. Perhaps she is so physically abhorrent that the only way to get me here – on this, our first date – was to conceal her appearance from me until the final moment in which we meet.

A shudder wracks my spine and I perform a merry little jig that would make an Irishman proud. I glance around the street, but nobody is watching. Thank God. I check my watch, just to make sure that her absence is due to my eagerness to arrive early and not her reluctance to show on time. It confirms that, no, she's not late, not yet, and I have a few more minutes before she is due. I start pacing back and forth between here and the bus-stop at the end of the street.

I ponder lighting a cigarette but don't, in case she finds it to be a turnoff. I'm feeling the need desperately though, and it is only exacerbated by the nervousness I'm feeling. I have mints, and so light a cigarette with the knowledge I can at least freshen my breath afterwards.

Somewhere, off in the distance, dopplering sirens pursue criminals across the concrete landscape. Other than that, I don't hear a thing until a voice breaks me from my reverie.

"You must be Michael."

I instinctively toss my half-smoked cigarette to the curb and turn. What strikes me first is how beautiful the woman standing in front of me is. Her long, brown hair dances on the breeze; her emerald green eyes implore me to respond.

"I am," I manage, though my throat is dry and I'm not sure even I understood the two simple words that fell from my lips. Luckily, she did, and she extends her hand for me to shake. What I truly want to do, though, is lean in and kiss this Goddess standing before me, before she changes her mind and is gone forever. "You're Keli."

I shake her hand. No, that's not enough, so I pull it slowly to my lips and kiss her knuckle tenderly. She smiles nervously, as if my gesture is just about on the right side of appropriate.

"I'm so sorry about the umbrella thing. I completely forgot, and I was worried you wouldn't recognize me." I'm babbling, but she doesn't seem to mind.

"There aren't many men standing around looking petrified," she says, scanning the street with that gorgeous smile of hers. Oh, that smile I could die for.

"So what do we have planned?" I ask. I have no idea and I've always thought it right to let the woman choose.

"I know a great little place, serves the best food."

"Sounds perfect," I say. "Lead the way."

We walk along the canal-side as we discuss our pasts, and I find myself leaving out more than a few things. I try not to stare at her as she speaks, but it's grueling and I keep finding myself absorbed in her profile. I don't think she notices, and even if she does, is she really going to tell me? I decide it's for the best if I turn my attention to the ground and kick tiny rocks along as she waxes lyrical about her current job.

"This way," she says, pulling me by the arm into some tight passageway between the buildings. I unsure exactly where we are; perhaps I should have been paying attention instead of side-footing pebbles.

"Isn't that a dead-end?" I ask as she yanks me further into the mystery space.

"It's this *way*," she repeats, as if that should satisfy my trepidation.

A few hundred meters away, I hear children shouting, no doubt embroiled in some must-win game of football. I hear them for only a moment before Keli – my new Goddess friend – grabs me by the back of my head and pulls me in for a kiss. It's a shock, but not wholly unwelcome. Our lips are perfect together, but then I taste blood and I realize her teeth are scratching at my lips.

I wince, try to pull away, but it's no use. She pulls me tighter, and now I'm gargling on the blood in my throat. If my tongue is still connected – which I'm not sure it is – I can't feel it.

A few seconds thereafter pain merges into a strange and soothing pleasure. She releases me and I fall backwards, cracking my head on the concrete as I land. Keli towers over me; her lips sodden with my blood; her eyes glowing with a fury I will never be able to comprehend. Their appearance makes me feel docile somehow, and I have no desire to resist her.

She drops to her knees and begins to feed. The pain only lasts for a moment or two; after that, I lie there and listen. I listen to the sirens dopplering in the distance and the children, well, they must have settled their argument or finished their game. Either way, their shouting has now ceased. The fading sirens in the distance are the last sounds that I will ever hear…

38. SKIN SIN
Shaun Avery

I stare up from the operating table, my consciousness returning to my body in sickly waves of grey.

My body.

My two favorite words.

Excited by the thought of what the surgeon has done to me, I try to pull myself up and off the table.

But I realize instantly that something is wrong.

There's an aching pain in the skin over my stomach.

"Doctor Daniels?" I say. "Where are you?"

No reply comes.

My sight is still coming back to me, my head not quite with it yet.

"Doctor, what's going on?" I say. "I didn't ask you to do anything to my stomach."

This is true. Bigger breasts, plumper lips, eyes with more 'come to bed now' in them, higher cheekbones, a rounder bottom, a smaller nose, and one of those fancy things they can do to make the lips of your vagina better, all of that I asked for – but I never mentioned the stomach. Why would I? It's always been perfectly flat and toned. And if he's done anything to it, I'll sue.

Well, I won't. Actually I *can't*, thanks to the form he had me sign. But I'll certainly give him a piece of my mind. That much I can stand to lose.

I manage to sit up on the table, and as my eyesight returns to full strength I look down at myself.

And that is when Doctor Daniels arrives.

"My God," I say, looking first at what he has done to me and then to the Doctor himself. "What the hell is this?"

"Yes," he says, looking at his handiwork. "Interesting design, isn't it?" He smiles. "Not something that you asked for, of course. But once you were stupid enough to let me put you under, I could do whatever I wanted to you."

"How dare you call me stupid?" I say. "I want a refund."

And I try to stand.

But some unseen force seems to be pinning me down.

Holding me back.

"It used to be enough," he says, "to paint a pentagram on the floor if you wanted to call forth demons. But times change. Now we have to carve them into skin."

He takes a step back.

The invisible power that keeps me trapped on the table is coming closer now.

I can feel it.

"I'm not even a real surgeon," he says. "This place is just a closed dental office I rented for a week and made up to look like a surgery."

I feel sick now.

And still I can't move.

"All I had to do was fool you," the Doctor goes on. "And with your naivety and vanity, that wasn't very hard."

He looks at the design he has carved into my skin.

The scalpel still bloody in his hand.

"But let me congratulate you on becoming a gateway," he says.

I look at him.

Tears stream down my face as I realize what is about to happen to me.

"Temporarily, at least," he says.

And then only overwhelming pain as something black and monstrous is bursting from my stomach.

39. THE SINCEREST FORM OF FLATTERY
Rick McQuiston

When Claire saw the woman, the first thing she felt was anger. Confusion quickly replaced the anger however, followed closely by the strongest emotion of all: fear. She set her cup of coffee down so hard that some of it spilled onto the table. It took her only a few seconds to confront the woman.

"What do you think you're doing?" Claire asked while biting her lip to keep from shouting. "I've seen you following me all around town. And every time I see you, you're wearing the exact same thing I'm wearing." She glanced at the woman's hair. "And now your hair is the same color as mine. Yesterday it was darker. Now it's lighter, just like mine."

The woman merely stared at Claire, her head tilted to the side ever so slightly.

"Well? I'm waiting for an answer. Or do I have to call the police?"

Still no reply came from the woman. Her eyes roamed over Claire's body, as if she were studying her.

Claire had had enough. She snatched her cell phone from her purse. "Fine, have it your way."

"Wait," the woman suddenly said in a calm voice. "I understand your anger, but if you interfere, the consequences would be dire."

Claire stood there, utterly confused. The strange woman who'd been following her, who looked disturbingly similar to her, was now asking her not to interfere?

"Please," the woman said, "if you will come with me, I will explain everything."

Claire didn't know what to say. She didn't know the woman at all. For all she knew the woman was a serial killer or a member of some bizarre cult.

The stranger set her purse down (an identical one to Claire's) and looked Claire in the eyes. An instant connection was made, joining the two women in an inseparable bond.

Claire couldn't move.

"Put your purse down."

Claire put her purse down.

"Now follow me."

Claire followed.

***

When she came to, Claire found herself strapped to a chair. A single bulb hung from a long wire above her head. It only illuminated four or five feet around her. "Hello? What am I doing here? Hello?"

A lone figure slowly emerged from the shadows.

"Hello, Claire."

It was the woman. She stepped up to Claire, again studying her look-a-like.

"Please," Claire begged, "let me go. I won't tell anyone. I have a family. I have children."

The woman smiled. "I know," she said quietly.

Claire grew flush with anger. "My husband will come looking for me! He'll find me and drag you straight to the police!"

"Oh, I doubt that." A few uneasy seconds passed. "You see, Claire, Michael will have no idea that anything has happened to you."

"H…how do you know my husband's name?"

"Because he's my husband. Now I want you tell me how to please him, or do I need to learn that on my own?"

Confusion swirled with the fear and anger already present in Claire's mind.

The anger won out.

Adrenaline coursed through Claire's body and gave her strength she never knew she had. In the span of a few seconds she was able to break free from her bonds and knock her startled abductor to the floor. Her small fists rained down fierce blows repeatedly, quickly reducing the woman to a unconscious, bloody heap.

Claire stopped her assault in mid-swing. She looked down at her victim and felt a sudden sense of remorse come over her.

But she didn't have time for that. She had to escape. She had to call the police. She had to call Michael and make sure her children were safe. If only she could find her cell phone.

And then something caught her attention. She bent over the still form of the woman and carefully lifted the sleeve off her left arm.

The blood…it was black! A thick black stain similar to molasses was seeping from the woman's wounds.

Claire straightened up. Her heart fluttered heavily in her chest. Something was very wrong, and not just because a strange woman had kidnapped her. No, something much worse, something that wasn't natural.

The woman on the floor began to twitch then, and with lightning speed, grabbed Claire's ankle.

***

Michael took a sip of his coffee and glanced at the clock on the microwave. "Hmmm…she should've been back by now."

Brushing aside the worry that threatened his good mood, Michael looked out the window and into the backyard. He watched his two children frolic on the swing set.

Claire stepped into the kitchen at that moment. "Hi Honey, I'm home."

Startled by her sudden appearance, Michael knocked a glass from the counter as he turned. It shattered on the tile floor.

Claire stooped over and began picking up the broken pieces.

"I'm sorry, Claire, I didn't hear you come in."

Claire looked up at Michael. "It's all right, Honey." A jagged shard from the glass sliced into her finger. She immediately covered it with her other hand.

"Are you okay?" Michael asked. "Here, let me see that."

Claire pushed his hand away and quickly left the room. "It's nothing," she said as she scurried to the bathroom. "I'll get a band aid for it." She touched him lovingly – longingly – as she passed him to leave the room.

Michael stood there, confused and upset. Claire was acting strangely. He walked over to the stove and pulled a small dish towel off the handle, and as he crouched down to wipe up the spilled coffee, something caught his eye.

There was a black substance on the floor. It looked like molasses.

40. LIQUID: A Flash story from Enlightened by Darkness

Robert Friedrich

What happens when the tender fabric of reality begins to tear? When everything that is defined and understood suddenly becomes less and less plausible? Where will you be at that moment, and what will happen to you?

For one man these questions would be asked presently. It was at first a regular day for a regular Joe, who sat silently in his arm chair reading the newspaper. But his world was about to turn to the unusual and the extreme.

As he sets down his daily paper, he sniffs at the air. The scent of smoke and burning flesh is about, as if a meal were burning in the kitchen. But there is no one else present who could be cooking, for he lived alone in his house. He then stands and walks around his small home, looking for the source of the peculiar aroma.

As he searches, the odor grows in intensity. Baffled, he continues to look around, until he notices smoke rising from his clothing. Somehow he cannot feel it, but his skin has begun to smolder. With shock he realizes that he is roasting alive, even as each new second passes.

The smoke continues to rise and his clothes begin to darken; his body is burning and he doesn't feel any pain. He runs to the bathroom and throws himself into the bathtub. Once the water hits his body the pain suddenly engages. The burning becomes more intense, and his nerve receptors now transmit all effects of the searing heat. He screams and rolls out of the bathtub, onto the bathroom floor.

Crawling upon the tile he cries and screams for help, and all the while he is aflame. His body hair is now gone and his features become unrecognizable. Both panicked and naked he crawls with desperation, as the scorching heat intensifies and his flesh is melted away. Before his vary eyes he begins to drip in flaming droplets upon the floor. His seared flesh falls upon the tile, slowly detaching itself from his muscles and his bone. His teeth begin to fall out, and his muscles atrophy and liquefy. He screams and shrieks as his interior tissues emerge from the charred outer shell, as he writhes upon of the blackened remains of his former body. Finally he collapses and dies; his entire bodily tissues, from skin to bone, having nearly melted away.

And then the final stages begin as smoke rises from the puddle of molten liquid left behind. The liquid begins to vibrate, and as the smoke clears, a new figure emerges from the bloody mess. Slowly, a creature forms from the deconstructed tissue that had been shed.

The creature rises from the bloody remains, and becomes visible as a female form. It is a naked woman that emerges from the bloody liquid as the smoke from the extinguished flame still swirls upon the ceiling. She is complete, beautiful, and naked; feminine perfection and every man's dream. She opens her eyes and slowly steps away from the charred remains and bloody liquid that has pooled upon the floor. She looks about the apartment and then halts suddenly. A devious grin appears on her lips as she steps through the doorway, and the room behind her bursts into searing flames.

41. EVIL JIMMY
Michele Tallarita

That morning, Jimmy locked himself in his room.

"Open this door!" Pam, his mother, yelled. *This child is evil.* She hated herself for thinking it. What child was evil? He was difficult, that was all.

She'd told him earlier, "Jimmy, I have a very, very important meeting this morning. Please don't make us late."

And he'd locked himself in his room.

Pam slapped the door with her open hand. The meeting was for her promotion, a promotion she needed. Her family of three was barely getting by. They desperately needed the pay bump.

"Jimmy, *please!*" she shouted.

Her daughter, Angie, looked up at her with wide eyes. Angie was so good, so sweet. How was it possible for her and Jimmy to emerge from the same sets of genes?

"It's alright, Angie," Pam said, looking at her watch. It was 9:02. She would already be late.

"Why does he always have to do this?" Angie said.

Angie was nine, two years older than Jimmy. *She sees he's evil, too.* A horrible thought. Of course Jimmy wasn't evil.

Except Pam was afraid to leave her two children alone. Whenever she did, she came back to find Angie cowering against a wall. Jimmy would be sitting on the floor, pushing a truck back and forth, looking perfectly innocent. But Angie would run out of the room crying.

Jimmy opened the bedroom door. Pam fell forward. She'd been leaning on it.

"What is the matter with you?" she shouted.

She grabbed the boy by the wrist and pulled him down the stairs. Jimmy was small for his age, but smart, according to his teachers. *They see it, too.* There was always a certain fear in their eyes when they talked about Jimmy. There'd been accidents in his classes, children whose fingers were crushed between desks, who wet their pants in the coatroom. The teachers never blamed Jimmy, probably couldn't prove he'd done anything. But there was that fear in their eyes.

When Pam lifted Jimmy into his seat, she saw that his jeans were soaked at the crotch.

It was 9:08.

"Damn it, Jimmy!"

She carried him back inside, made him change, refused to leave the room in case he locked himself in again. She shouldn't have mentioned the meeting. He was doing this on purpose.

Angie was crying when they got back in the car. Sometimes Pam wondered if she should beg Jimmy's father to take him, for Angie's sake. Her brother was traumatizing her.

"I'm sorry, Mommy," Jimmy said when they were halfway to the school. He sounded so innocent, so sorrowful. Maybe he wasn't evil. Maybe he was just a little boy with behavioral problems. Her little boy, her Jimmy.

"It's alright, Jimmy," Pam said. How would she pay next month's rent, without the promotion?

A minute later, Angie cried out. "Ouch!"

Pam couldn't look back; this was a tricky intersection. "What's going on back there?"

"Ouch!" Angie said.

"Jimmy, whatever you're doing, stop it!" Pam said.

Angie kept shouting. Pam got onto an easier road and then craned her neck to see what was going on.

Jimmy was sitting with his hands folded, his expression smug. Angie was crying loudly.

Pam lost it. "I'm sick of you, Jimmy! I'm absolutely sick of you! What is the matter with you?"

She never saw the truck coming.

A crash, blackness, a wailing ambulance. Pam's head throbbed. She was flying. No, she was lying on a stretcher. Fluorescent light panels streamed above her.

"My children!" she cried.

A woman in white leaned over her. "Stay with me, Pam."

"My children!"

"Don't worry about them right now."

She couldn't feel her legs. Couldn't feel them at all. "Oh, God!"

"Pam, stay with me."

Blackness, again. Voices whispered around her about spinal fractures and blood loss. She swayed in and out consciousness.

This is your fault, you know. It was Jimmy's voice, in her head. She screamed, but the scream didn't get beyond her own mind.

Don't you remember? he said. *The deal you made?*

What deal?

His laughter echoed on and on.

There had been a deal. She'd forgotten it, until now. It had been such a small thing, a tiny thought she'd had. She'd been nineteen, insanely in love with a man who was with another woman.

If I could have him, she'd thought, *I'd do anything.*

Another voice in her head, an evil voice. *Would you bear my child, not yours?*

I'd do anything.

The other woman disappeared. What had happened to her? Pam never asked. But within a week, the man she loved asked her on a date, despite never having noticed her before.

Did he leave Pam and the children because the whole thing had never been his choice?

Of course not. It was his choice. What was she thinking?

She woke up gasping. "My children! Where are my children?"

"Pam, calm down." The nurse touched Pam's shoulder.

"Tell me where my children are!"

"Not until you calm down."

Pam forced herself to take deep breaths. Her neck was in a brace. She still couldn't feel her legs.

"Pam," the nurse said, forehead lined, "only one of your children survived the accident."

There was laughter in Pam's head.

"Which one?" Pam choked.

"Jimmy passed away on the way to the hospital."

Pam's tears shook the bed. Two more nurses rushed in with a sedative. She was going to make her injuries worse.

"He was the son of a demon!" she sobbed.

"What is she saying?"

Blackness, again. Angie was alive, and Jimmy was dead. She hated herself for thanking God.

***

Angie sat quietly, arm in a sling, watching Pam sleep.

"Will you be alright alone for a minute, sweetie?" the nurse said.

"Yes," Angie said.

The nurse smiled sadly and walked off.

Adults could be so trusting of cute children.

Angie watched Pam's chest rise and fall. The girl wouldn't kill her; Angie didn't want to end up in a home. Jimmy was the one who'd had to go. He'd been useful, for a time, but soon he would've outgrown his usefulness. Would've told people about the voice in his head, making him do things. Her voice. A seven-year-old believed everyone heard such a voice, but an eight-year-old did not.

What fun she'd had. And now she had Pam's complete confidence. Angie my good child, Angie my sweet child. Hyuk.

Didn't she know that true evil hid itself until the right moment?

One day, when it would cause her the most pain, Angie would tell Pam her good child had died when he was seven. That he'd begged the voice to stop making him do things.

But the daughter of Satan would bide her time.

42. CROSSROAD BLUES
Marc Sorondo

Robert tossed back another mouthful of bourbon and surveyed the crowd that filled the small roadside bar. Between the hot, moist air and the alcohol, he was covered by a film of greasy sweat. It dripped from under the brim of his black fedora and down his face, ran off his cleft chin and fell like big droplets of rain that splashed on the glossy surface of his guitar.

He decided he had time for one more song. He knew just which one he would do. He stepped up to the microphone and strummed once. The crowd quieted but did not fall completely silent.

> I met a black dog at the crossroad
> Late one hot summer night
> I met a black dog at the crossroad
> And his eyes were full of light
>
> Midnight where the paths cross
> The master made his play
> Made a deal where the paths cross
> For the gift, I'd gladly pay

Robert closed his eyes and played a few bars, bringing notes that should have been impossible from his cheap old guitar. Then he stopped playing, put his mouth back to the microphone, and wailed:

> I was due back at the crossroad
> Soul to take, life to steal
> Instead I ran from the crossroad
> Black dogs at my heal
>
> The master's coming for me
> And I'll be damned when I'm caught
> Someday he'll find my sorry ass
> But I'll smile and know I fought

Robert stepped back, struck a series of wailing chords. Then he let his last song die.

The crowd was silent except for a single figure clapping slowly at the back of the bar. The figure stood in a shadow, face hidden in darkness, but his eyes glowed with the fire of knowledge. No one else in the bar turned and looked to this man who clapped from within the shadows. It was as though none of their senses could detect him...

Robert realized then that he'd lingered too long, and that his time had come. The talent that he'd bartered for remained, but the patrons could no longer perceive it. It was as though he were, in body and soul, somehow dead already. A futile attempt certainly, but he decided to run anyway...to run until the very end.

43. THOSE FOUR WALLS
Justin Hunter

It all comes down to Cheerios and those four walls. The baby was delightfully numb. He would rub his fingers over the mesh of his port-a-crib. Faster and faster, he would rub until his fingers burned from the friction and his senses ran into overdrive. He would hesitate for a moment and let the feeling pass, then rub again - Over and over and over. If he stopped rubbing everything would stop.

There was nobody there to talk to him. There was nothing in the crib except a soiled blanket. There used to be a yellow and pink stuffed bear as well. He had thrown that over the top of the crib days ago. Nobody had placed it back in.

The silence was too much of a void, so he would rub and rub and rub. The mesh wove patterns of light as his fingers raced back and forth. Millions of rays played a game of light and shadow. Sometimes he would get lost in them. He could get so involved that he would just stare at the little holes. Those were the best times. It was like he wasn't even there.

There were times when he found his voice. He would shout louder and louder. The air would expel from his lungs. His muscles would tense with the joy of it all. There was no purpose to it. Just to make noise was enough. The volume pounded in his head, giving him a headache. He could push everything else away with the sound.

He would close his eyes tight and a torrent of white and black spots would dance in the darkness behind the shut lids. The sound of his squealing would sometimes bring something else. Something beautiful or painful - It was only a matter of time.

Sometimes she would come. Staggering with eyes closed from light and pain. Heavy hands would land on the frayed edges of his port-a-crib. She would regard him and he her.

If only he could stop screaming for a moment. But he found that he could not. He would scream and scream. Sometimes she would tell him to shut the fuck up. Sometimes she would hit him. It made no difference. The screams would come from somewhere inside of him. They were as regular as breathing and as normal as his beating heart.

And there were the moments of silence. Sometimes a slap would come so hard that screaming was impossible. The spots in his vision would become swirling stars and skin dazzled in explosions of sharp pain.

After, there was a tingling numbness as he sucked in air. Not enough for another scream. Focus came back as often as it did not. When it did, she was gone.

Sometimes when she came it was different. She would coo and pick him up. His body would tense against her touch. So much in his little body wanted to press into her. To feel her skin. To be close to her.

But there was something in her touch that repelled him as much as it drew him. He found himself fighting against her, pulling at her hair, biting her. Sometimes she would throw him back into the crib and be gone again. Sometimes she would place him on the ground on his back. She would take off his foul and dripping diaper, clean him and put on a new one. She would tell him that he smelled like shit. She would say he was disgusting. She would tell him she wished he was dead.

He couldn't look into her eyes. There was so much he didn't like to see there. He would lie on the floor, let her clean him, avoid her eyes and concentrate on the touch. It all comes down to Cheerios and those four walls.

Sometimes he would drop. Legs just didn't work after awhile. He would lie very still and look toward the ceiling as it spun and spun and spun. She would lounge on the couch and pick her nose. Sometimes she would forget to take the needle out of her arm, and it would bob with the motion of her hands. She stared and stared, smiling all the time, nothing behind her eyes.

He would cry sometimes. The pain in his stomach would make him cry. She would drift off the couch and move to the kitchen as if in a dream. She would get the yellow box and float back toward him. Then the rain would come. Small tan circles poured into the crib, bouncing off his face, arms and body. He would open his mouth and some would drop in. The crunch was perfection.

He would crawl through his stained and foul crib and eat every piece of cereal he found. Sometimes she would only drop in a little. The best times were when the yellow box would slip from her fingers and fall into the crib. It would all be his. Then he would sleep. When he awoke, he found his legs worked again and he could stand up.

"I have to shit," she said. "Oh, man I have to shit so bad. Where's the fucking bathroom? I have to get to the fucking bathroom."

She stood up and wobbled grotesquely, bumping against the wall as she staggered to the bathroom.

"Shut the fuck up," The man would say. "You're just coming unplugged from all that shit. It has to happen sometime." He laughed and laughed.

He rubbed his fingers over the mesh and watched her.

"Go and get some more shit," she said.

"I think I will," The man said. "I don't want to be around when you come unplugged anyway." He walked out of the house and closed the door.

She pulled her pants down and slumped onto the toilet and shuddered.

The baby rubbed the mesh on the port-a-crib, trying to leave and get lost in the light. But he couldn't; he had to watch. He had to be there.

"Oh, shit. Holy shit," she said. She lifted her body off the toilet and it tensed as her body shoved forward. A baby dropped from her vagina, cradled in a wet weave of afterbirth. The tiny body thumped on the bathroom tile.

She stood there looking down at the baby. The umbilical cord still snaked into her. It looked like a grey dead snake. The tiny baby cried. So did she.

All of a sudden the flickering light from the mesh caught his eye, and he was lost in the sparkling light. He could feel the heat from his fingers rubbing back and forth, faster and faster. It goes away. It makes everything go away.

44. STAY SCARED
Rick McQuiston

"So," Ricky said quietly, "the only way to avoid her attention is to stay scared."

Jeff, a diminutive kid who was frightened of his own shadow, pulled his blanket up over his chin. "That won't be a problem for me," he mumbled through the fabric.

Mike laughed. He was a good-natured boy who had been one of their club, The Three Musketeers, for the last five years.

Ricky grew serious. "Mike, I'm not kidding around. The Musketeers have to stick together."

"I know, I know," Mike replied almost casually. "Take it easy." He reached over and pulled yet another candy bar from his backpack. It was his third one in the last hour.

Ricky nodded. "We need to shore up the fort in case she comes." He waved his flashlight around the makeshift structure.

Jeff turned around. "No problem." He reached back and pulled the sheet taut.

"Good," Ricky said. "And make sure there are no openings anywhere. She can squeeze through even the tiniest hole."

Mike took a bite of his candy bar. "So what are we supposed to do if she comes? I mean, how will our fort keep her out?"

"I already told you guys," Ricky replied with irritation. "All you have to do is stay scared. If she thinks you're scared of her, she'll leave you alone. It's like some sort of weird thing with her."

Jeff finished securing the sheet behind where he was sitting. "Are you kidding us, Ricky?"

"No, she's real. She's like a walking nightmare. She's got long black tentacles instead of arms, and teeth so sharp that she cuts some of her own tongues every time she closes her mouth."

Jeff's jaw fell open. "Tongues? She's got more than one?"

"Yeah, and each one is covered in scales."

Mike finished his latest candy bar. "But we're just three kids hiding in your bedroom in a fort made of boxes and bed sheets. If this monster is real like you say it is, then were as good as dead."

Ricky shook his head at his friend's doubt. "All you need to do is stay scared." He glanced at his watch. "It's almost ten. She usually shows up around 10 o'clock."

Jeff was scared. Even if what Ricky said was true, and his being scared would save him, it still didn't make him feel any better. "What is she?" he asked through his fingers.

Ricky shrugged. "I don't know exactly. One time she looked just like my sister. Another time, Ms. Pressly from English class. This time she might look like one of your moms, or Madonna, or even Martha Washington. Who knows? I think she's some kind of demon who picks certain kids to haunt. She wants to keep them scared of her. If they aren't..." His expression grew long.

Mike snickered. "How come you know so much about this demon?"

"I don't know, maybe because she picked me to haunt."

The bedroom door creaked open at that moment. A lone figure entered the room.

"It's her. It's her," Jeff mumbled. He was terrified.

"That's good," Ricky said in a hush. "You're scared. And so am I." He looked over at Mike. "Remember, whatever happens, stay scared." He clicked the flashlight off.

Mike nodded. He gripped his blanket with white knuckles.

The figure stood in the darkness for a few minutes. It said nothing. It did not move.

"We're gonna die" Jeff sobbed.

Ricky tapped his friend on the shoulder. "Quiet! You'll be all right. She won't hurt you."

The figure glided through the room. It approached the fort without a sound, and brushed a hand across the fabric.

"Ricky, I don't want you boys staying up too late. Your father has to get up early in the morning."

"That's no demon," Mike said. He grabbed the flashlight and clicked it on. He started fumbling through his bag for another candy bar. "It's only your mom. You were pulling our chain all along."

Ricky grabbed the flashlight from him and immediately shut it off. "No! You have to believe! You have to stay scared!"

A black tentacle sliced through one of the bed sheet walls at that moment and wrapped around Mike's throat. Six more tentacles then slid in through the same opening, and with a powerful jerk, pulled him out into the darkness.

An uneaten candy bar fell to the floor.

Both Ricky and Jeff stared wide-eyed at the empty space where their friend used to be.

"It pretended to be your mom!" Jeff whispered through clenched teeth. "It tricked us into not being scared of it."

Ricky tried to hide his smile. "I warned him," he said quietly. "I warned him."

He enjoyed helping out his friend sometimes. The demon told him once that prey tastes so much better when at first it's afraid and then isn't.

Ricky covered his mouth to keep from chuckling. The demon would reward him generously for executing the plan so perfectly. He wondered what she would get him this time.

45. THE MEMORY OF LOVE
Peter Adam Salomon

It snowed the day she came back into my life. A late fall storm that blanketed red and gold leaves with white sugar icing. It had been humid and gray the day they'd buried her.

Today, as snow fell upon a sea of maple, her voice whispered against me. The heat began in my heart and shot outwards, bleeding off my fingers as memories called to me, my name on her soft lips. Outside, the storm continued, but I couldn't see through where my breath had fogged the window. When I turned around, she was perched on the edge of the bed, waiting for me to join her.

Blonde hair curled over her shoulders, blue eyes stared through me, drawing me in. When she reached for me, I fell to my knees in front of her, pulling her against me. The exquisite feel of her burned through me. I had forgotten how soft skin could be, how sweet the breath shared in that first kiss, how wonderful she was, how alive and beautiful and mine.

She was gone when I awoke, though her scent lingered. As it always had. That first kiss still wet my lips, the taste of her on my tongue. I dragged myself away, refusing to look behind me to see the empty bed. I couldn't help myself, I never could. I looked.

She was perched on the edge of the bed, waiting, once again, for me to join her. There was nothing else but her, smiling at me and with each step I took towards her, that glorious smile grew. She was waiting, willing. Oh, so willing.

Blue eyes pierced me to the core as her memory called my name. Soft, sweet, beautiful, wonderful, I had never stopped missing her. Not when I buried her. Not in all the days since. There was a vast emptiness within where she had been. I missed her, still. I missed her, always.

I remembered watching her die, holding her in my arms as she drew that last precious breath before she left me. Alone. Forever alone. Now, it was snowing and, once more, I held her in my arms. She kissed away each tear that slid down my cheek, banishing the nightmare that had been her death. Promising me that I'd never be alone again. That she'd fill the void I'd lived with for so very long.

With her whisper-sweet voice, she invited me to join her, to never miss her again. To never be alone. To be with her. Forever. Always.

That she finally wanted me as much as I had always wanted her. She was there, waiting. Waiting for me. After all these years, living through the nightmare of my life without her, she'd finally forgiven me for killing her.

And all I had to do was die.

46. THE EGG SAC
Ken MacGregor

It was warm for the start of spring, and the sun shone through fluffy white clouds and onto a little girl playing in her backyard. A small, wiener-shaped dog tagged along at her heels, stubby tail wiggling. Helen Thompson was playing Tinkerbell, jacket unbuttoned, the bottom flapping out to the sides like wings. She was waving around a twig she'd found and was casting spells all over the yard. She turned Arnold the dachshund into a pony and filled the round, plastic pool with green Jello. Next, she made the whole house purple, her favorite color. She was entranced with the details of her make-believe game.

Helen skipped over to the fence that bordered the yard. She fully intended to turn it into a castle moat filled with alligators and sharks. That would be a good way to keep Bobby-the-Booger next door from bothering her. He had such a stupid face!

In a corner of the fence, Helen saw something peculiar. It made her forget all about Bobby. It was a white something-or-other just about eye level with her as she stood. It was stuck to the fence, tucked back, nearly invisible until she was near. If Helen hadn't come up from the angle she had, she never would have seen it. It looked like some kind of bag or sac, filled with something mysterious. She raised her magic wand.

Helen poked at the sac with the long twig. The stick caught on the gooey surface of the organic tissue. She wasn't sure, but she thought it might be spider eggs. It looked like the picture of the one in "Charlotte's Web," a book her Dad read to her at many bedtimes. She imagined hundreds of little aeronauts sailing away, waving at her, calling to her in their tiny voices. *Goodbye, Helen! Thank you! Salutations!* Helen smiled at the thought. She lifted the sac, still stuck on the twig and carried it inside. It was bigger than the one in the book. No way could Wilbur fit this in his mouth!

Helen went straight to her room, hiding the sac in her closet. It was early March, so she figured the eggs would hatch in the next month or so, just like in the book. She couldn't wait to meet all her little spider friends.

She forgot about the egg sac within a week.

***

Helen and Vicky, another first-grader from the neighborhood, were playing Go Fish in Helen's room. Helen couldn't stop staring at Vicky's

136

strawberry-blonde hair. It was shiny and silky like an American Girl doll's hair. Helen's own hair was mouse brown and she hated the way that her mother had them cut it. Six years old, and already the fires of jealousy smoldered in her heart.

"Go fish," Vicky said. Turns out she didn't have any tens. Helen reached for the pile, spread out face-down in a sea of cards to choose from. Her hand stopped, distracted by her ears. There was a sound like ripping paper towels coming from the closet. Vicky heard it, too. Both girls looked in the direction of the sound. Suddenly, Helen remembered the egg sac. She smiled. It was so cool that Vicky would be here to see this! Helen stood up and did an excited little jump.

"It's okay," she told Vicky. "I know what that is. Watch!" Helen strode to the closet and flung open the door in a *ta-da!* fashion. She watched Vicky's face for a reaction, just knowing the little balloonists would come flying out on the breeze. It made no difference that there was no breeze in the room. When you're six, imagination is everything.

Vicky's eyes got huge. For a moment, she just stared at the open closet. Then she screamed. It wasn't a cute little-girl scream. This was pure terror formed in an instant. Helen was confused by this reaction, and leaned over to look for herself.

Helen's closet had a small dresser in it full of toys and art supplies which she rarely used anymore. There was a dollhouse in there, too; it was broken, a little dusty. Helen's winter boots were piled on the floor, four pairs. She had a real passion for boots of all kinds. She knew all this was in her closet, but couldn't see any of it. Spiders, brown and black the size of acorns covered every surface. Thousands of segmented legs wriggled on the walls, floor and ceiling. The little girl shuddered as the creatures scurried toward them with surprising speed.

Her bedroom door then burst open and in ran her father. He stopped and stared, trying to process what he saw. Vicky saw her chance and took it. She ran from the sea of rapidly approaching spiders, dodging around Mr. Thompson's legs and through the open door. She screamed on down the hall.

Helen's dad scooped up his daughter into his arms, pulling her back from the arachnid horde. He frantically brushed them off her arms and legs while carrying her from the room. He was only seconds too late. The tiny creatures were caught in Helen's clothes; they were under her arms; far too many for her father to get them all.

The bites hurt terribly, more than anything the little girl had ever known. Tears streamed down her face, and her jaw clamped shut against the pain. Helen whimpered into her daddy's chest. He held her to him and cursed as he too was bitten. She could feel a burning, and then numbness spread throughout her body. Her dad stumbled, caught the wall, and then fell to one knee. Helen looked at his face; it was twisted with pain.

"Daddy," she whispered, "I'm sorry. It's my fault." Her father mumbled something in denial, but it was indeed her fault and she knew it with certainty. And as the numbness consumed her completely, she had a final fantasy about tiny, friendly spiders spinning words into webs. *Some Girl! Terrific! Radiant!* Helen's mind was growing fuzzy. Her vision blurred. She clung to her daddy, who clung back as hard as he could. Both of them were fighting to stay conscious… to stay alive…

A spider crawled by Helen's face, mandibles opening and closing, like it wanted to be fed. Then, it joined the writhing mass of furry bodies heading down the hall. Downstairs. Mom was down stairs. The front door was downstairs. The rest of the world was downstairs… Guilt consumed her. She felt about as far from terrific and radiant as anyone could. Next to Helen, her father took short, labored breaths. His skin was turning an unhealthy greenish color. She never meant to hurt her daddy. She never meant to hurt anyone. She closed her eyes and regretfully accepted that the egg sac had sealed their doom…

47. SKRATTI
Nicholas Paschall

The German winters were always harsh on those who had settled in the peaceful valleys of the Wetterstein portion of the Alps. The grandmothers would bleed chickens before preparing them for supper, mixing the blood with foxglove and barley to ward away evil spirits, while the men would go in groups to tend to the sheep and the cattle, or to hunt. The children would stay indoors with their mothers and aunts where they played or helped with chores.

Josiah hated chores.

He hated chores almost as much as he hated the foul smelling glop his grandmother would smear upon his forehead every night before bed, *"to keep the Skratti away!"* Josiah didn't believe in the old fairy tales of imps and fairies, despite the claims of the old men of the village who swore that they had seen the nasty little humanoids. They were said to be a clan of malevolent dwarves who resided within the dark section of forest to the East. Beware to anyone who entered their domain...

Josiah looked up from his stool with his brilliant emerald eyes, where he'd been whittling away at a length of Maplewood, creating a proper sword. His mother smiled down at him.

"Bed time!" She crooned, smiling widely as she scooped him up off the stool, into her big arms and bountiful chest. "Come on my little warrior, your sword can wait until another day."

Josiah didn't argue out of fatigue. Earlier he had asked his uncle to show him how to use a sword properly, and they'd spent several hours engaged in the lesson. Josiah had used a dulled dagger (he was but six summers old, not fit enough for a proper blade). His uncle had corrected Josiah's posture and stances while the youth stabbed and hacked at a stump. Never before had he grown so tired!

Snuggled beneath the leathery furs of his bed that night, he pulled away from his grandmother as she attempted to smear the mixture of blood across his crown. For minutes she tried, pleading with him to behave and do as he was told, until she finally relented from exhaustion.

"Fine! Be a fool and take a risk!" She threw her hands into the air with disgust, stomping away to apply the admixture to the other children. Josiah merely smiled and drifted off to sleep, proud of his victory over the old hag.

Josiah awoke not to the gentle musings of his mother, nor the yelling of his younger siblings, but to the jostling of his mattress as someone climbed on. Emily, his youngest sister of four, would often leave her own crook and come to his bed on cold nights. So he thought nothing of it, and held up the blanket and commanded at the darkness for her to get under and be still. The entity hurried beneath the pelt with a high-pitched giggle, while Josiah merely rolled over and attempted to fall back into sleep.

His last conscious thoughts were of the quiet crooning song being whispered into his ear not by his baby sister, but by some impish honey-voiced witch…

"Hush young one,
To Eden, you'll come;
Your days of life,
Will be undone.
The Skratti have need,
And only come by,
When invite is granted
Upon you to feed."

The next morning was met with the shrieks and wails of Josiah's mother and grandmother, for when they had gone to rouse him from his slumber, they'd found only a bloody mess where his bed had been. And a trail of smeared gore leading all the way to the far wall, as if a dead animal had been dragged. The grandmother, her gnarled hands quickly shucking away the ruined pelt, wailed even louder upon finding a small doll made of straw and hair, with green pebbles for eyes the same color as Josiah's.

The Skratti never took without payment, the grandmother thought bitterly as she looked at the rough jade stones lodged in the strange little doll. The Skratti were unlike man in that regard; while we had more food than we could handle, the Skratti horded the rare gems and gold of the earth. So they chose to trade it for their favorite food, so long as it signaled itself to be willing.

She realized with both horror and relief that the remaining children of the village were now assured to accept her protections before they slumbered…

140

48. BLOODLESS
William Holden

What causes the mind to sour?
Isolation?
Paranoia?
Fear?

Whatever the reason - I'm know I'm losing mine. I can feel my brain curdling like month-old milk. The stench is weeping through my pores. The pungent, putrid scent is starting to suffocate me. I imagine that my brain is nothing more than lumps of greyish-white matter, festering, fermenting, and souring inside of my head. It feels as if it's swelling, building pressure inside my skull with its liquid, clumps of rot. I worry that if it continues to expand, hairline cracks will form in my skull allowing the putrid mess to spill from my head and seep from the pores of my skin.

What began as a simple passion for the body has become much too dangerous. The searing heat, the painful pleasure, and the rush of letting go has consumed me. The force is dominating my emotions, manipulating my desires, and controlling my thoughts. The only way that I've found to fight back is to write everything down and chase the darkness out of my mind and purge it onto the page. I need the words to cleanse my body, my mind, and my soul of this sick, demented force that I cannot see, nor fight with any conviction. My desperate efforts to bathe in my words are suffering the same death that I fear will soon be mine. As the ink dries, the effects dissipate. The cravings always return. Each time the need is stronger - more desperate than before.

I look out across my room. It is hollow, empty of life itself. The only movements are a continuous cloud of smoke from my cigarettes, and a broken traffic light outside my window. The flashing light causes the room to shift and change. It washes my walls, my body, and my mind with its blood-red pulse. It beats against my eyes, over and over - never stopping. It has become a part of me... of part of what I am becoming.

My ink runs dry. The efforts of my written words go unnoticed. I set down my fountain pen. In its place I pick up the razor. My body quivers with anticipation of another cut, another draw, another dip of the silver nib of the pen. I look for a clean, unblemished spot on my arm. I find one just below the wrist. I watch with growing fascination, eagerness, and horror as I slip the edge of the blade into my flesh. The silence of the room allows me to hear the skin being punctured with a sickening pop. The razor slips easily into the tissue. I drag it across my arm. The skin tears with a smooth edge. The skin peels back ever so slightly, like a small bloody mouth of a goldfish begging to be fed.

My body tenses, and then relaxes. A chill rushes over me as if I have begun an orgasm, causing the vein in my arm to spasm. The blood bubbles out of my arm like vomit boiling on a hot burner. The red liquid gathers around the old scars of my arm creating little rivers of life flowing from my body. I dip my pen into the cut. I let the pen absorb my body's ink. I begin to write again. The endless process starts once more. With each refill of the ink, I slip further into the darkness, becoming nothing more than a bloodless body, desperately trying to write away the growing evil that has taken me in its grasp and refuses to exit my body.

49. SELF HELP
Raymond Gates

Relax. Breathe. Just keep telling yourself, it's only pain. It's only pain.

I've been afraid of pain for as long as I can remember. Agliophobia, the grand procession of experts call it. That's about all they agree on.

They've all speculated about why I have this fear, of course. Everything from Battered Child Syndrome to Oedipus Complex. Interesting, if somewhat imbecilic theories. Daddy never beat me, and I've certainly never had sexual feelings for my mother.

Hotplate's on. Stay calm. Breathe.

Being the youngest of three, some might think I was given special treatment as a child. Rubbish. My parents clothed me, fed me, and attended my hygienic needs, but were otherwise indifferent to me. I was educated, though without praise or encouragement, and disciplined, though not in any physical sense. I believe I was raised as any average child of the time would be.

My siblings, though. Well, that's a different matter.

Everything's soundproofed. No one will hear anything.

Hannah was Daddy's darling. She was almost in her teenage years when I was born. She always sat on Daddy's lap. Their combined shadows would dance across the wall under the glare of the television. Daddy had strong, calloused hands to hold her with. Sometimes those hands slipped beneath her blouse, or the waistband of her shorts. She'd squirm and do her best not to whine; it didn't take much to turn those hands to fists. She never cried out, even though it obviously hurt sometimes. After a while, she didn't even cry.

It was my fifth birthday when she ran away.

Gauze. Bandages. Where's the disinfectant? I'm sure I... There it is.

Our brother was four years younger than Hannah. Michael was, for the most part, ignored by Daddy. Our mother wasn't much better, and even her minor attentions diminished after I was born. He hated me; hated all of us, I believe. I don't remember Michael ever hurting me, but I was always afraid he would. He hurt Hannah sometimes. Thumbtacks on chairs, centipedes in her bed, that sort of thing. He broke her arm once, at a playground. She fell from the top of a slide they were on. An accident, he claimed. A lot of accidents happened around Michael.

To this day I don't understand why he kept doing it. The welts from Daddy's belt, the black eyes, and the cigar burns seemed to far outweigh any sort of satisfaction he must have felt. When Hannah left, I thought he'd start on me, but he didn't.

I often wonder how it felt when Michael dropped the fan heater into his bath.

Heart's racing. Relax. Focus on something else. Look. The tongs are changing color as they heat up. Pretty whorls of purple, blue and yellow.

Daddy disappeared after Michael died. Just left for work one day and never came back. Mother descended into a kind of bipolar state. She'd smother me with affection, and then berate me as the cause of her pain. She tried to home-school me for a while. Her Prozac and bourbon cocktails meant I spent more time ensuring she didn't choke on her own vomit than studying.

It's ready. Roll up your sleeves. Relax. Breathe. It's only pain. It's only pain.

Without the internet, I don't think I would've survived. The online world's a wonderful thing for someone like me. Information at your fingertips. Online education. Everything is accessible with a login and a credit card. I've become quite adept at accessing information. With a normal life, I probably would've been a programmer, or an analyst.

Use the oven mitt. See? There's heat, but no pain. You're fine. You're in control.

I've spoken with doctors, psychiatrists, pain specialists, anyone who might give me a cure for my condition. I've devoured the latest research, gone through case histories, and examined all the treatment options. Medication, though obtainable, doesn't seem wise. Alternative therapies seem useless. I did find something amongst the cognitive therapies that holds promise though.

It's called Progressive Exposure Therapy. The idea is to gradually expose yourself to the thing you're afraid of. Start with talking about your fear, then try looking at a picture of it. Progress towards having it in the room with you. Spend time with it, until you can bear to move close and embrace it.

It usually takes months, even years, to achieve success. I'm going to try and fast-track the process.

You're a little sweaty, a little shaky, but you're doing fine. Relax. Breathe.

It was easy enough to find him. There aren't many places a man like Daddy can go. The suggestion of mother having an insurance windfall, however false it might have been, was a tasty enough lure to bring him back to the house. Mother doesn't know. She's semi-comatose most of the time now.

A little diazepam laced coffee, a little physical exertion, and I'm ready for my treatment.

He's coming round. Check the straps. Tight. Secure. Good.

I hold the tongs poised between his naked thighs, like some metallic bird of prey. He doesn't seem to know whether to cry or curse. They say it helps if you visualize things that make you calm. Overcome the negative stimulus with a positive one. I try to picture Hannah's smile. I try to think of a time when Michael played with me. I can't recall either.

My hand trembles. Daddy begs. I close my eyes, and the tongs. There's a pungent smell. Daddy screams.

I know this is the only way I'll get better.

Just breathe. It's only pain. It's only pain.

50. SCORNED
Winifred Burniston

She had thirty minutes to get rid of the body and the fucking shovel was stuck. It was the folding, military kind left over from her husband's last deployment and it had been conveniently within arm's reach as the bitch had tried to leave. Gina had snatched it up and swung like she was in the majors, cracking Natalie above her left ear as she'd turned back for a final comment. Whatever Natalie was planning on saying was forever silenced as her jaw broke from the impact. Her eye popped out at the same time with a sickening smack, dangling down onto the crimson ruin of her face. Unfortunately, she didn't have the good sense to just die, instead running around shrieking, flapping her hands and mangled jaw as she bled all over everything.

Gina reached back into the milk crate of tools and sporting equipment where the shovel had been and grabbed an aluminum baseball bat. When Natalie chicken-flapped by again, Gina bashed her head repeatedly until the noise and movement stopped. Flinging the slick bat towards the bulkhead stairs, she bent over the crumpled mess at her feet and attempted to wrench the shovel out of the corpse's skull. It just wouldn't budge.

"Goddamnit!" she hissed after looking at her watch. Thirty minutes until Rick got home. She'd checked his flight, everything was running on time, and barring any traffic issues, she was screwed. She was covered from head to toe in blood and gore and the basement resembled a slasher film set. This wasn't what she'd planned, not by a long shot. Gina had invited Natalie over to scare the shit out of her, to get her to walk away from Rick and the sleazy affair they were having. She'd brought Natalie into the basement on the pretense of getting the laundry out of the dryer. She'd known there was going to be screaming involved. She'd wanted to do this on her turf, where she felt secure and strong, but she hadn't wanted the argument overheard by the neighbors.

Natalie hadn't been fazed at all by her yelling or threats. She'd laughed. The bitch had laughed in her face! And then she'd been stupid enough to tell Gina that Rick was leaving her once he got home from his business trip. He was going to tell her and move in with Natalie.

The rest of the screaming and name calling Gina couldn't really remember. She'd gone past hysteria and into a mental state she didn't recognize. She'd known the tears streaming down her face weren't of sorrow or pain, but of pure, acidic rage. Gina trembled as she rode the adrenaline wave coursing through her veins. Natalie grossly misread Gina's reaction as weakness and fear. So, she'd lobbed her verbal coup de gras, clearly expecting Gina to collapse in an emotional heap.

"What the hell did you expect, Gina? Rick likes his pussy hot, not flash frozen like yours!"

That's when Natalie's face had erupted in a rush of brains and blood as the steel blade sliced into her cranium. And although the noise Natalie had made registered with Gina, it couldn't override the unearthly sound inside her own head. A low howl grew with each second she'd spent listening to that woman, until it reached a fever pitch shredding what remained of her coherent mind. Now, Natalie was dead and her lousy, cheating husband was on his way to the scene of the crime.

"What do I do now?" she wondered. Looking around, she saw a bunched up tarp jammed onto a storage shelf. Grabbing it, she shook it out like a bed comforter, settling a few inches away from Natalie's feet. Gina grabbed Natalie's ankles, hauling her onto the material leaving a roadkill swath of blood on the concrete in her wake. Gina rolled the tarp over the body as best as she could, the shovel's handle still sticking out of the package. After dragging the bundle to the bulkhead stairs, she was ready to focus on the cellar. Starting for the inside stairs to get cleaning supplies, she stopped before putting her hand on the railing. It was covered with incriminating evidence, which she shouldn't spread to anything else, especially the upstairs. She stripped down to her underwear and bare feet. Dropping the clothes and shoes by the tarp, she headed up the bulkhead to the safety of her secluded backyard.

The air was cool and still as the icy water from the hose stung her skin. Damp hair hung in her eyes as she scrubbed drying blood from under her nails. Turning off the hose, she checked her watch again. Amazingly, only ten minutes had passed. With a wet dog shake, she headed back to the mess in her cellar.

Twenty minutes wasn't enough time to dispose of the body. She stripped off the wet underwear, adding it to the growing pile of evidence, pulling out a towel and some clean clothes from the dryer. She was almost dressed when the phone rang. Frozen to the spot, it took a moment for her to remember to breathe. She dashed up the stairs, snatching the receiver off its cradle.

"Hello?" She heard the tremble in her voice and inwardly cursed.

"Hey, Babe, it's me, everything okay?" It was Rick. And suddenly her mind cleared. She knew what he was going to say next. He wasn't coming home tonight. How many times had she heard this before? She trembled anew with rage. The bastard wasn't just screwing around; he really was planning on leaving.

"Yeah, sorta got a mess here, but what's up? You gonna make it home tonight?"

Now it was Rick's turn to be flustered. "Uhmm, no. My flight got delayed until tomorrow night. What's going on there?"

Gina smiled and said, "The washer overflowed in the basement and I'm going to have to spend the night cleaning up the mess."

She barely heard the rest of Rick's chastising her about too much detergent and overloading the machine. Hanging up, she walked out to the yard, to drive Natalie's car around back. She and Natalie were going on a little road trip, back to Natalie's house. That's where she was sure Rick was going to be, if he wasn't already there.

It was a cute little cottage, surrounded on all sides by conservation land and deserted woods. No nosy neighbors to bother the festivities she was planning. After she got Natalie's body into the car, she'd go get Rick's service revolver from the bedroom and his chainsaw. The basement could wait until after her little welcome home party for her husband.

51. *Bonus Tale* THE BOX
Matt Drabble

Patrick Riven clutched the box as tightly as he dared. The large plastic container seemed strangely cold to the touch and he couldn't help but feel a sense of dread as the box's weight pressed heavily into his lap.

He was a heavy set man of 56 with an overly generous waistline and a bushy bearded face that had seen better days. His hair was a dirty blonde in all senses of the word and it had been a long time since a pair of scissors had trimmed his locks.

The bus rounded a corner a little too sharply and the box almost slid from his grasp. Something rolled and thudded heavily against the side of the container and for the thousandth time in the last hour he wondered what was inside.

The job had been simplicity itself with careful instructions that left no room for misinterpretation. He was given two addresses, one to pick up and one to drop off. The only other rule was that under no circumstances was he to look inside.

He had been drinking in the bar past closing one night. Rudy the bartender had taken pity on him and had only been charging for every third drink or so. Apparently some guy had been in after closing the last couple of weeks looking for a courier.

The man had finally made an appearance last night as Patrick had been drowning his liver. The old man was tall with a natty dress sense that seemed out of place in the dive of a bar. His three pieced suit was old fashioned, but in a classic sort of way. He wore a gold chain pocket watch which glinted under the bar's neon light and caught Patrick's eye. Such an accoutrement would no doubt fetch a pretty penny that Patrick could sorely use. As the man drew closer however all thoughts of robbery went out of his mind. The man was old, tall and thin, but far from frail.

"I understand that you have a job" Patrick had said conversationally.

The man responded by sliding a small white card across the bar counter. Patrick took the card. There were two addresses written on it. "Pick up here, drop off here" the man said pointing at the elegant handwriting. "The job pays ten thousand with only one condition, you never open the box."

"Not even a peak?" Patrick had joked.

"NEVER!" The man had snapped banging a manicured fist down hard on the bar. "You never open it. You will be watched from a discreet distance and I shall know if you have broken my rule."

"Alright, alright jeez," Patrick responded. "When do I get paid?"

The man responded by sliding an envelope across the mahogany counter. "Half now, half when you drop it off."

Patrick had eyed the envelope with hungry eyes. "Is it illegal? Is it drugs?" He'd asked with a dry mouth.

"For ten grand do you care?"

Patrick thought about the amount of bottles he could buy with ten grand and decided that he didn't.

He had picked the package up at the first address. It had been a rundown motel with no-one on duty. The plastic container had been sitting on the reception desk with his name engraved on a small card. The box was white with a blue lid and handle. There were four clasps on the lid with no discernible locks. The clasps would just snap open with minimal effort and Patrick stared at the box for a several minutes. There was a strange curiosity that stole over him. It was like being a child and getting told that you couldn't cross the road. Even though you never had any intention of doing so, suddenly the forbidden became the only thing that you could think about. He had stood staring at the box for what seemed like an age, before he had finally gotten his desire to look under control. For ten grand, he didn't want to take the risk. The old man had said that he would be under constant but discreet surveillance, and something told him it would be wise not to disbelieve him.

The bus chugged back into life and pulled away from the curb. Patrick noticed that a couple of teenagers had gotten on at the last stop and they were now eyeing the box with undisguised greed in their eyes. They were shabbily dressed with faded jackets, but both were lean and hungry.

The public transport route that he had to take to the drop off point was far from safe. This was an urban jungle full of predators and Patrick tried his best to look tough, but he knew that he was failing. His stop was two more down the line, and he hoped that the youths would get off before him. But hope was luck's second cousin and neither had ever served him well.

Just as he'd feared the two youths followed him off of the bus at his destination stop. The area was rundown and deserted. This was where the city had failed and all that was left was dog shit instead of tumbleweed.

Patrick suddenly ducked down between two buildings and followed the narrow path through the overgrown weeds. He made a couple of quick turns whilst trying to keep his bearings. His drop off address was a building about a quarter mile across the docks and all he had to do was lose his pursuers.

He doubled back on himself and circled around again, all the while keeping a sharp ear out for the teens. He was congratulating himself when he stepped out of the shadows and ran straight into the back of one of the boys, before falling to the ground.

"Hey old man, been looking for you," the teen sneered.

"I don't want no trouble," Patrick said from his sitting position in the dirt with his hands up as the box lay at his side.

The second teenager turned the corner and smiled cruelly as he spotted their prey sitting helplessly on the ground. "Well now isn't this pretty," he grinned.

"I got some money, here," Patrick pleaded, thrusting his wallet towards them. "Just leave the box alone," He realized his mistake as both of the boys turned to stare at the plastic container.

"What's in it?" The first boy demanded.

"You can't have it," Patrick said stridently as he reached out and grabbed the box.

The second teen stepped forward and kicked him hard in the ribs with nonchalant ease. The first boy slipped his hand into his faded jacket and drew a black handled knife that glinted viciously in the light. The boy knelt down and Patrick could smell his foul breathe up close. The knife touched his cheek and the boy pressed down hard enough to draw a single droplet of blood from his flesh. Patrick thought of the one slice of good fortune that had been bestowed upon him, and the certainty that a couple of kids were going to take it away. It was his box, his box dammit.

He reached up without thinking and grabbed the boy's knife hand. The teen was so accustomed to getting his own way with mere threats that he was slow to react. Patrick twisted the knife and pushed it up and under the punk's chin. He shoved hard and the blade slid into the boy's throat like it was butter. The teen's flesh tore open and Patrick's hand was soaked with blood. He leapt to his feet fuelled with adrenaline and charged the other. He drove the knife into the boy's chest over and over again panting like a wild animal.

When he stood back he looked down to find his shirt soaked with blood and he wanted to scream to the sky in victory. It was his box and no-one else was going to take his prize away.

He walked slowly back to the container that was lying on its side. He righted the box and his hands trembled as he touched the clasps. Surely if the old man had indeed been watching then he would have stepped forward to save his precious cargo. The logic seemed faultless and Patrick now felt certain that he was alone.

His fingers shook as he popped the first clasp. Surely after everything he had done to protect the box he was entitled to a look, just a peak to satisfy the gnawing curiosity that wormed in his guts. Before he knew it the rest of the clasps were snapped open and the lid was loose. With a shaking hand he pulled it off and stared inside at a severed head and a pair of dead eyes staring back at his.

"Isn't that a pity," a voice startled him from behind.

He turned to face the old man standing behind him with a sad expression.

"Who is he?" Patrick asked, but feared the answer.

"Your predecessor," the old man answered.

Patrick turned back to the box only to find it now empty. "I don't understand."

"You will," the old man replied as Patrick felt the touch of sharp steel pressed against his neck.

To be continued in…

**Demonic Visions
50 Horror Tales
Volume II**

www.ingramcontent.com/pod-product-compliance
Lightning Source LLC
Chambersburg PA
CBHW070613120726
47909CB00004B/1209